VOL. 4, NO. 3   **ISSUE #15**

FEATURES

NEW STORIES

FIRST PUBLICATION

FROM THE CAT'S PERCH

There are many organizations for crime fiction writers—Crime Writers' Association, International Thriller Writers, Mystery Writers of America, Private Eye Writers of America, and Sisters in Crime, among them—but only one specifically for writers of short crime fiction: the Short Mystery Fiction Society (SMFS).

The SMFS is a loosely run organization founded in April 1996 when the members of Margo Power's shortmystery-l changed its name to better reflect membership's goal of representing mystery and crime short stories. The organization has grown and changed over time, and the current membership includes writers, editors, publishers, and fans of all subgenres of short crime fiction.

In 1997 the SMFS established the Derringer Awards, which are awarded exclusively to short fiction. First presented in 1998, the Derringers have been presented annually ever since. The SMFS also presents the Edward D. Hoch Memorial Golden Derringer for Lifetime Achievement to a living writer who has "produced an impressive body of short crime fiction, and [has] made a major impact on the genre," and honors deceased writers' impact on the mystery and crime short story with the Short Mystery Hall of Fame.

Learn more about the Short Mystery Fiction Society at https://shortmystery.blogspot.com and join by visiting the Group.io page at https://shortmystery.groups.io/g/main and following the directions.

If you write short crime fiction, you need to be a member.

—Michael Bracken
Editor, *Black Cat Mystery Magazine*

Staff

PUBLISHER & EXECUTIVE EDITOR
John Gregory Betancourt

EDITOR
Michael Bracken

WILDSIDE PRESS SUBSCRIPTION SERVICES
Carla Coupe

PRODUCTION TEAM
Sam Hogan
Karl Würf

ARMADILLO BY MORNING

STACY WOODSON

Roy pulled into the gravel parking lot, took a sip of his gas-station coffee, and stared at the animal shelter's red brick building. It was hard to believe next week there would be no afternoon shifts, no nights on call, no animal rescues.

He'd be retired.

Roy wasn't leaving his job bitter like most retirees. He was grateful. After returning from Vietnam, the animal control job had been just what he'd needed—a chance to preserve life rather than take it. But now his body was deteriorating, and all he wanted to do was get through these last days with some dignity.

He glanced at his rescued Great Dane in the passenger seat and smiled. "Guess we better get inside, old girl."

Lulu barked, and Roy got out of his truck. When his feet hit the ground, pain shot through his body. Wincing, he shifted his duty belt, so his bite stick and pistol weren't pressed against his bad hip, and made his way to the building. Lulu followed at his heels.

Roy hoped today would be slow. Maybe he'd write a few license citations, find a loose dog, administer some vaccinations. Nothing too crazy so that he and Lulu would be home in time to watch reruns of *Columbo*.

After Roy walked through the kennels and greeted the dogs, he went to the office to check in with their dispatcher, Pauline, a woman nearly as old as Roy. With her wild hair and raspy voice, she reminded him of Phyllis Diller. She sat at her desk, a pack of Lucky Strikes next to her computer, a game of solitaire on the screen.

"Morning, Pauline."

"Roy." She popped her gum, not bothering to look up from her game.

He walked past Pauline's desk through a cloud of tobacco, spearmint, and drugstore perfume.

Lulu sneezed, then pawed at her nose.

"Your dog alright, Roy?"

"She's fine." Roy scratched Lulu's ears. "Aren't you, girl?"

Lulu barked.

Roy continued to the table where they kept their radios and grabbed one from the charging station. Next, he went to the storage locker and pulled out a tranquilizer gun and a rifle.

He was loading his work truck when Pauline came over the radio.

"Armadillo by Morning."

Her melodious tone reminded Roy of the George Strait song with a similar name, and he found no humor in it. He knew who had requested field service—a cantankerous old bat named Millie Wendell.

Unfortunately, their jurisdiction just touched her property near Morning, a small town on the outskirts of Smith County. Roy was there nearly once a week, and Millie Wendell's crazy was the kind he wanted to avoid today. He ignored Pauline, continued to load his truck, hopeful if he waited long enough another officer would respond.

"I know you're out there, Roy," Pauline scolded. "Saw you pick up that radio."

He groaned before he finally keyed his walkie. "Still got a few things to deal with here," he lied. "Can't Nash take the call?"

"Nash is on the other side of the county dealing with a skunk."

He tried to come up with another solution, something that didn't include him driving out to Morning.

But he had nothing.

"Roy?"

"Copy that," he said, reluctantly.

Pauline gave him the address, not that he needed it. But it was protocol, and Pauline was big on protocol—unless it involved talking on the radio or playing solitaire or smoking in the bathroom.

"Come on, Lulu," Roy said. "Let's go see what Millie's armadillo tore up, now."

Lulu barked, like she always did when Roy spoke to her. Then, she jumped into the truck and scrambled across the seat to the passenger side.

After Roy stopped at the hardware store for supplies, he headed east on TX-31. Suburban box stores and small-town neighborhoods turned to trailer parks and open stretches of land with occasional billboards—the most recent about the Texas Rose Festival.

An annual event held in Tyler, there was a parade, a gardening competition, and a festival queen, which Millie won decades ago. Even after all these years, she still acted like this entitled her to something.

Her only redeeming quality was her husband, Stan.

Roy drank beer with Stan on Bingo nights at the VFW. He was broken like Roy, always showing up with something stitched or bruised. Stan was a decent guy. Short on judgment marrying the likes of Millie. But everyone had some cross to bear, and old Millie seemed to be Stan's.

In the distance, Roy saw the sign for the Wendell property. The last time he serviced one of Millie's calls, she attacked him with the garden hose, and he dreaded what Millie had in store for him today.

Roy made the turn and followed the long dirt road to a two-story house. The ornate moldings and trim made the house look Victorian—the kind of house you'd see on Main Street, not something you'd see in the middle of nowhere.

Once, over beers, Stan told Roy that Millie liked to claim their house was a historic landmark even though it wasn't listed on the National Register. She had one of those bronze plaques engraved and made Stan hang it by the door. She boasted about the house's supposed provenance at church, telling fellow parishioners Sam Houston had slept there. She'd even convinced their pastor to feature the place during their candlelight home tour. But the attention on Millie and her faux historic home was short-lived, foiled by Luanne Johnson. Another former festival queen and Millie's rival, Luanne's *real* historic home had been featured in the *Home and Style* section of their local newspaper.

Roy had laughed when he'd imagined Millie's reaction to the article.

But not Stan.

Not that day. He'd stared at Roy, eyes haunted, sucking down his beer like he wanted to drown a bad memory.

Mind still on Stan, Roy pulled up to the Wendell house. He waited, hoping his friend would hear the engine idling, walk outside, and maybe he wouldn't have to deal with Millie.

Unfortunately, luck wasn't on his side today.

"Here goes nothing." Roy left the engine running so the AC would be on for Lulu, put on his Stetson, and climbed out of the truck. He winced from his hip, but continued to the porch, trying to ignore the hitch in his gait.

The front door was open, but the storm door was closed. In a last-ditch effort to avoid Millie, Roy edged back his hat, put his hands above his eyes and pressed his face against the window, hoping to see Stan on the other side.

His friend's cane was propped near the door, but he wasn't with it.

"Crap." Roy sighed. He stood on the porch a few seconds longer before he finally steeled his shoulders and lifted his hand to knock—until he heard Millie ripping Stan a new one.

He leaned closer to the door. Even turned up his hearing aids. But he could only make out a few words, cuss ones, mostly.

He considered leaving. He could tell Pauline no one was home. Hell, he could even lie and say he'd completed the service call. But in the end, he knew it wouldn't matter. Millie would call again, and he'd be back out here anyway.

He started to knock again, but stopped short when he heard a sickening sound—the bwak, thud, bwak like something you'd hear in a boxing ring.

Jesus.

Roy grimaced.

Had Stan finally snapped and walloped Millie?

He didn't seem like the kind of guy who would strike his wife. But Roy watched the Crime Channel and had seen good men pushed to the edge by their crazy wives. Then, it was bwak, thud, bwak, hello prison.

"Millie," Roy called. "Y'all okay in there?"

When she didn't answer, Roy yanked at the door, but it held tight against the frame. The silence continued—the silence more unnerving than the tussle he'd heard earlier.

He imagined Millie sprawled on the floor, Stan leaning over her battered body. But the shriek that followed wasn't Millie's.

It was Stan's.

Roy reached for his duty belt. Yanked at the bite stick. Aimed it at the glass door. Swung back—

And Millie appeared. "Damn time you got here."

Bite stick still raised, heart still jackhammering, he stared at Millie.

There were no bumps or bruises from what he could see. She wore a yellow apron over her standard white button-up shirt and khaki pants. Her hair, normally pulled into a tight bun, was unaccustomedly loose. Otherwise, her appearance looked no different than any other day.

"Cat got your tongue, Roy?"

He returned the bite stick to his duty belt. "Morning, Millie."

"Been nearly an hour since I made that call. Is this the kind of service my tax dollars pay for?" She smoothed her apron, and blood trailed behind her hands.

Roy frowned. No visible cuts, no bandages, no sign she was injured. Things just didn't make sense.

He continued to stare while Millie continued to rant.

"You all come moseying out here whenever you damn well please. Some glorified welfare system the government is running at that animal shelter, if you ask me. I have a mind to call the county supervisor and complain."

"Stan okay?" Roy finally asked.

Millie pushed the storm door open, spring sputtering, and joined Roy on the porch. "The armadillo is what you should be asking about, not my sorry excuse for a husband."

"Just the same. That was quite a ruckus I heard, and I'd feel better knowing he was okay."

Her eyes narrowed. "Stan ain't the one who made the call, Roy."

Millie sidestepping questions wasn't something new. If the conversation wasn't a topic she found interesting, she usually changed the subject. But Roy wouldn't let it go, not today, not when Stan may be hurt.

"Be happy to check on that armadillo for you, Millie, *after* I see Stan."

A muscle in Millie's jaw flickered. She glanced toward her garden where the armadillo had likely struck again.

If she denied his request, Roy wondered if his hip would hold when he pushed past her and forced his way inside. Thankfully, Roy didn't have to test it.

Millie shot him a withering look and yelled, "Stan!"

Feet shuffled against hardwood floors. The storm door whined, and his friend joined Millie on the porch. Instead of his cane, he held a blood-stained dishtowel against his forearm. His eyes were haunted like that day at the VFW.

"Morning, Roy." Stan flashed a strained smile.

"Stan." Roy hooked his thumbs on his belt. "Looks like a nasty cut you got there. You okay, man?"

Stan opened his mouth to say something, but Millie interrupted. "That man has no business being in the kitchen. You won't believe what he—"

Roy cut her off. "I want to hear from Stan."

Stan's eyes darted from Roy to Millie, and his face flushed. "You know me. Always doing something to myself."

"What was it this time?" Roy pressed.

"Man against cantaloupe." Stan gave a hollow laugh. "Tried to cut the squirrely thing, but it got away from me."

Roy thought something was squirrely, all right. And it wasn't fruit.

Millie folded her arms. "Now, if you're satisfied, Roy…"

He wasn't. There was a twinge in his gut. The kind of feeling he used to get when he was on patrol in Vietnam right before an ambush.

"You may need stitches. I could take you to a hospital." Roy offered, hoping to talk to his friend alone.

"Thanks," Stan said. "But there's no need. It's just a scratch."

"If you all are done playing nicey-nice, I have a garden that needs some attention."

Roy opened his mouth to say something more, to find a way to get Stan to reconsider his offer for medical aid, but Stan had already turned back to the house.

Alone with Millie and out of options, Roy followed her down the porch, past his truck. Lulu shot him a sympathetic look from the passenger side window. He wished he could climb into the truck and leave with her.

A few strides later, Roy reached Millie's garden. The lush lawn had sections of rose-filled flower beds with beautiful blooms that were almost at their peak. The ground appeared soft and moist, the perfect mix for Millie's armadillo.

"So, what seems to be the problem?" Roy asked, reflexively.

Millie's face twisted. "Are you blind?"

Roy was, nearly. He wore glasses with thick lenses and black frames— the kind soldiers called birth control glasses because they were ugly enough to repel women. When he took them off, the world was a blur. But right now, his glasses were on, and he could see the armadillo's damage just fine.

"You see it now?" Millie pointed toward the pushed-up section of dirt—cone-shaped pits three to four inches deep—remnants from the armadillo's recent food expedition. "Damn thing is tearing up my flower beds, again."

"It's a cryin' shame," Roy said, and he meant it. The flowers were beautiful.

"I don't need your tears. I just need you to kill the damn thing."

"It's like I told you before, Millie, I can't kill something I can't see."

Each time Roy serviced one of her armadillo calls, the varmint was never there. Today was no different. Even if the rooter were right in front of him, he wouldn't kill it. The armadillo was just trying to survive, just like Roy, and it wouldn't solve Millie's problem, anyway.

Trapping and removing it wouldn't help either. In both instances, another armadillo would just take the current culprit's place. The only way Millie could fix her problem was to attack the animal's food source, which is what Roy had told her the last time he was here—the same day she'd blasted him with the hose. He tensed at the memory.

Roy quickly searched for the hose, prayed it wasn't near Millie, and found it next to a thick cluster of bushes with something metal that glinted in the sun—the spigot, no doubt.

He eyed both warily. "Did you try killing the grubs like we talked about?"

"You think I have time to wait for that pesticide to work? The Rose Festival is a week away, and I'll be damned if this year's gardening award goes to Luanne Johnson."

Millie pulled a pair of pruning shears from her apron pocket.

She had already attacked him with the garden hose, were the shears next?

Roy's hand went to his pistol.

But Millie didn't attack.

She walked past him to a rose bush and snipped away a wilted bloom. "Fix my armadillo problem, Roy."

He had a fix. The same fix Millie didn't like. But he went to his truck anyway and grabbed the grub killer he'd picked up from the hardware store.

Lulu eyed him from the passenger seat.

"I know," Roy said to the Great Dane. "Probably going to go over like a fart in church." He just didn't know how to make it clearer to Millie that taking away the armadillo's food supply was the only way to stop it from digging in her garden.

Lulu barked when he shut the door. He wasn't sure if it was because she agreed with him or simply to wish him luck. It was tough to tell with Lulu.

He returned to the garden where Millie was still pruning and set the box of pesticide next to her. "Some varmints need to be put down, Millie. Your armadillo ain't one of them."

When Roy climbed into his truck and pulled away, Stan peered at him through a second-floor window, eyes still haunted. And the twinge in Roy's gut returned—just as the box of pesticide sailed through the air and exploded against the hood of his truck.

* * * *

At work the next day, things were slow. Roy spent most of his time in the kennels. A few of the dogs had to be spayed or neutered, so he took them to the animal surgery center. The whole time, he kept thinking about Stan.

Roy considered checking on him, but Stan didn't have a cell phone. The house phone was an option, but Roy wasn't confident Stan would speak openly with Millie around. So, he decided to wait, knowing he'd see Stan at Bingo night.

But Roy was wrong.

Stan never showed at the VFW, and he went home—his wallet a little lighter, his heart a little heavier—concerned about his friend.

At his house, he slipped into his La-Z-Boy, Lulu at his feet. He contemplated calling the Wendell place again. But the last thing Stan needed was Millie raging over a late-night call, and he decided against it. So, Roy traded his phone for the remote.

Too late for *Columbo*, too early for the Crime Channel's *Murder by Midnight*, he settled on Animal Planet—an episode featuring armadillos, and he laughed at the irony. He listened as the host discussed their migration patterns, food habits, and their armor-like skin that reportedly inspired weapons researchers to create protective material of similar design. The boring commentary was enough to lull him to sleep.

Hours later, Roy awoke, neck stiff. He looked at his watch. It was after midnight and time to go to bed. But instead of turning off the TV, he clicked over to the Crime Channel. It took Roy a minute to get his bearings, the show already in full swing.

It was another domestic abuse case. This time, the victim was a man.

"Men are taught never to hit women," a man named Clint said. He wore a prison jump suit and sat in front of a metal table. "I couldn't fight back. And I couldn't stop what was going on." He talked about how he'd been too embarrassed to call the police, worried what others would think. How, when he'd finally found the courage to ask for help, he wasn't taken seriously, despite his visible injuries. "Grow some balls," one cop had said. "You can't handle your old lady," another had complained.

"It's just a scratch."

The words echoed in Roy's head. Hadn't Stan said the same thing?

Clint continued to talk about how the system failed him, how he eventually snapped.

Roy cycled through memories of Bingo nights, Stan's never-ending cuts and bruises. His haunted stares.

Was Stan battered too?

The twinge in Roy's gut returned.

At least this time he knew why.

* * * *

On Roy's last day at work, more folks than usual milled around the office, and Pauline was actually friendly. He knew they had something special planned for his retirement, and he'd been looking forward to it. Until his recent revelation about Stan.

It was the only thing he could think about. Truth be told, he wasn't sure what to believe. Last night he was confident Stan was abused, but this morning the idea just didn't seem right. Stan was a military veteran, and the notion Millie could put a hurt on him seemed absurd.

Still, Roy had seen Stan's haunted looks, the cuts, the bruises. And there was that twinge in his gut. Logic versus instinct were at war with each other, and Roy wasn't sure which side to take.

He was still mulling through it when Nash approached him. His bald head glistened under the fluorescent lights, and he smelled like skunk.

Roy wrinkled his nose. "Should I ask?"

Nash shook his head. He pulled out a can of tobacco, slipped a wad into his mouth. "Big day for you. Any retirement plans?"

"Fishing. You know, the usual stuff," Roy said, dismissively, his mind still on Stan. "Curious, Nash. You ever respond to a service call at the Wendell place?"

"Who hasn't?" Nash pulled a discarded coffee cup from a wastebasket, lifted it to his lips, and spit. "You know how Millie is about them roses."

"Ever notice anything"—Roy paused and considered how much he should reveal to Nash. The last thing Stan needed were rumors circulating about Millie—"*peculiar*?"

Nash frowned. "Peculiar, how?"

"You know, with Millie."

"Woman is crazy as a jaybird and has a temper to boot—if that's what you mean by peculiar. Once, caught her running after Stan with a shovel. Smacked him square between his shoulders. Old boy collapsed like a house of cards."

Roy thought about his own experience with Millie's temper—the garden hose, the box of pesticide—and he could imagine how things may escalate at home.

"Is that all?" Roy asked, curious if there were more.

"Ain't that enough?"

It was enough for Roy.

"Of course, it's Stan's dang fault for marrying that woman," Nash continued. He spit into his cup again. "Guess we all have our crosses to bear, and Millie is Stan's. That poor bastard."

Roy's stomach tightened. He was guilty of thinking the same thing. Was this how they all justified Millie's behavior? That it was somehow Stan's fault?

He needed to talk to Stan. Face-to-face. Away from Millie.

And he needed to do it now.

Roy glanced toward the break room. The door was cracked, and he could see the streamers and balloons. He hated to disappoint his co-workers, but he had a friend in need and that had to come first. As luck would have it, Roy found an opportunity to duck out gracefully.

"Armadillo by Morning," Pauline said, her eyes on Nash, phone still to her ear.

"Speak of the devil." Nash smirked.

"I'll do it," Roy said, quickly.

Pauline popped her gum and eyed Roy.

"It's your last day on the job. You should enjoy it." Nash glanced toward the break room, leaned closer and whispered. "Pauline made chocolate cake."

"I do love chocolate," Roy whispered back. "The cake will keep, don't you think? Let me have this one last service call for posterity."

Nash frowned. "Sure, that's the kind of posterity you want?"

* * * *

Lulu followed Roy to his truck and soon they were on TX-31 headed east. They passed the same suburban box stores, the same small-town neighborhoods and trailer parks, the same stretches of land and billboards. It wasn't the advertisement about the Rose Festival that grabbed Roy's attention this time.

It was the billboard about the Domestic Violence Helpline.

There was a picture of two men—one head down, the other gripped his shoulders—with a caption that read: *Now is the time to help a friend.*

Roy wondered how many times he'd driven blindly past it, and how many others had missed it too.

Minutes later, he made the turn for the Wendell place. He followed the road to the driveway. Millie sat on the porch in her trademark khaki pants, white button-down shirt, and apron—this one blood-free.

No Stan.

Roy left the AC on for Lulu and climbed out of the truck. Pain shot through his hip. He gritted his teeth, shifted his pistol, and then continued toward Millie.

"Roy!" she exclaimed, her voice nearly giddy. "It's out there. The armadillo." She pointed toward her garden. "Stan's been keeping an eye on it for me. Haven't you, Stan?"

Roy turned and saw Stan in the garden, leaning against his cane. He looked tired, pain etched on his face. A bandage was on his arm from the "cantaloupe incident," and a fresh bruise was on his cheek.

Roy walked over to him.

"Morning," Stan said, his eyes still fixed on Millie's garden.

"You hearing what I'm saying, Roy?" Millie called. "The armadillo—you can *finally* kill it."

Roy turned his back to Millie and focused on Stan. "You alright, man?"

Stan's haunted eyes looked at him. "Why wouldn't I be?"

Roy had a list of reasons, but this wasn't the time to go through them. Not with Millie hovering nearby.

He tried to think of a way he could get Stan to leave, something Millie wouldn't think twice about, an opportunity to speak with him alone. "Folks are throwing a retirement thing for me at the shelter today." Roy tilted his head toward his truck. "Why not ride back? Have a little cake. Maybe we can grab a beer after it's over."

"I don't know." Stan looked back at Millie, making her way down the porch.

"The armadillo, Roy," Millie said, her voice flat, the joy gone.

"I ain't killing it, Millie."

"What do you mean you ain't killing it?" Her voice rose an octave. "You said you can't kill what you can't see. Well, the armadillo is right there. Show him, Stan."

Stan dutifully pointed toward a section of Millie's garden and the cat-sized animal waddling through it. The armadillo's armor-like skin, scales brown and heavy, nearly blended in with the dark soil. The varmint lifted its head, beady eyes half-shuttered. It sniffed the air and started to dig.

Roy didn't move.

"Now you listen, Roy. You listen close. I was the festival queen once and on my way to the Texas State Beauty Pageant. Until I eloped with Stan. Thought the man was going places with his fancy car and college degree. Look what it got me." She pointed at the ramshackle house with disgust. "Biggest mistake I ever made. Been spending my entire life trying to get back what that man took from me." She pushed back her shoulders. "You bet folks will take notice when I win this rose competition. And I'll be damned if some hussy like Luanne Johnson or some stupid armadillo is going to take it from me." Millie folded her arms. "You better do something, Roy. Because if you don't, God help me, I will."

"I did something," Roy said, an edge to his voice. "Each time I came out here. Ain't my fault you didn't like my solution. I've seen enough killing to last a lifetime. Rose Festival or not, I ain't killing that armadillo. Not when there's a humane way to get rid of it."

Millie's neck grew red and then her face. Wild-eyed, she balled her hands, let out a battle cry, and charged at Roy.

He stumbled back, his bad hip gave way. He waved his arms, tried to regain his balance.

But it was no use.

Lulu barked just before Roy crashed to the ground. Pain shot through his body—the kind of pain that made grown men vomit. He rolled to his side, curled into the fetal position, leaving his gun exposed.

Millie yanked it from the holster.

"Gun," Roy yelled, trying to warn Stan.

A round went off.

More pain.

Roy patted his body, searched for the wound. But the pain was coming from his hip. He looked for his friend and found him still standing, staring at Millie.

"Get down," Roy yelled, again.

But Stan didn't move. He continued to stare. It wasn't fear behind his eyes. There was simply nothing.

Another round.

Another miss.

Roy hugged the ground. His hearing aids whistled. Despite the sound, he could hear Lulu barking.

"Damn dog needs to shut up," Millie yelled. She pointed Roy's pistol toward the truck.

Roy's body turned cold.

Not Lulu.

He forced himself to his hands and knees. Tried to stand.

Millie fired.

Another round—this one hit metal.

The Great Dane whimpered.

Roy's heart hollowed out. "Lulu," he cried, desperate to hear her reassuring bark. He tried to look at the truck, to see if Lulu was injured, but Millie blocked his view.

Millie pointed the gun back at the armadillo.

This time Stan was moving, his face tight, the vacant look gone. Anger filled his eyes. He walked toward Millie, her focus still on the armadillo.

He raised his cane to swing.

Millie fired. Jerked back—

And collapsed.

Stan still stood there, cane still raised, eyes wide—almost as wide as the bullet hole in Millie's throat.

Stunned, Roy looked toward the garden, the same direction Millie had pointed the pistol and fired that last shot. The armadillo was still there rooting in the ground. The sun glimmered against the animal's armor-like shell that now had a black streak—residue from the bullet that had ricocheted and struck her.

Roy shook his head. He'd never look at an armadillo the same way again.

With the threat neutralized, Roy had to get to Lulu. He tried to stand, but his hip couldn't take it. He called her name, tried to whistle, his eyes fixed on the truck. "Come on, old girl."

He waited, hoped.

Prayed.

When the Great Dane jumped against the window, Roy nearly cried with relief.

Stan helped Roy to his feet. "You, okay?"

Roy nodded.

They glanced down at Millie, bleeding out, gasping for air. Roy reached for his radio to call for help, but stopped when Stan grabbed his arm and pleaded, "Please, don't."

Roy looked back at Millie. He thought about Stan, the hell she had put him through. The hell she would put him through again. Roy had seen enough killing, but he also knew some varmints needed to be put down, and Millie was one of them.

He released the radio.

Stan nodded his thanks before he shuffled toward the house. He stopped at the hose, reached deep into the bushes, and tugged out a small metal container—the same metal that Roy mistook for the spigot just the other day. Stan pulled off the lid, returned to the armadillo, and tossed a handful of grubs at the soil.

Roy stared, slack-jawed at what he was witnessing. Millie's source of misery—the armadillo—Stan had been feeding the varmint all along.

"There are different forms of justice," Stan said while he tossed the remaining grubs into the soil, "and this was mine."

The armadillo lifted his head toward Stan, and Roy could have sworn the old varmint smiled. ✗

Stacy Woodson (stacywoodson.com) is a US Army veteran, and memories of her time in the military are often a source of inspiration for her stories. She made her crime fiction debut in *Ellery Queen Mystery Magazine*'s Department of First Stories and won the 2018 Readers Award. Since her debut, her stories have been adapted for animation, won the Derringer award twice, selected for *The Best Mystery Stories of the Year 2024*, and nominated for a Thriller Award.

AFTER THEIR CONVICTIONS, SIX MURDERERS REFLECT ON HOW KILLING MR. BODDY CHANGED THEIR LIVES

TARA LASKOWSKI AND ART TAYLOR

Professor Plum, with the Dagger, in the Library

Please, no, really no need to call me *professor*. *Doctor* is fine. I've earned that, I'm proud of it, but *professor*... It has been so many years since I've graced a classroom. What university would have me after...everything? The accusation, the trial, the conviction, the...*incarceration*. My tenure track application quickly derailed, needless to say.

Readers—many of them, many just like you—have often asked whether I miss those hallowed halls, that ivory tower.

The answer is no. Give me *prison* again before that. No daily labor could be worse than lesson plans and stacks of grading, no chain gang more hardened than a faculty cohort, no world more cutthroat or existence more soul-crushing than...*academia*.

It's a moot point, though, whether I'd go back. Ha! What university could even *afford* me now?

But at the time, I didn't know that. At the time, tenure seemed the *only* thing worth working toward, really worth *living* for. That singular ambition lurked in the back of my mind every moment of the day, consumed my thoughts, directed all my actions.

My application, when the time came, was—I say this without hubris—exemplary. Solid teaching evaluations, exceptional even. Praiseworthy recommendations, I'm sure of it. And a track record of highly regarded scholarship, with a new book on the way.

So why did I reach out to Mr. Boddy? We had gone to college together, the university where I later taught, lived in the same dorm one year—friends once upon a time, I dare say, though more like acquaintances as his standing rose. Certainly, as a member of our alma mater's board of regents, he lived in a different world than an assistant professor like me, but we had some history together, and his family's philanthropy was well known. Wasn't it possible that he himself might show a little generosity my own way, for old times' sake?

So, I asked him to put in a small word on behalf of my application—unnecessary, I stressed, but appreciated. I even gave him an advance peek at my next book, then in peer review: *Spoofing Suspense: Parody in Crime Fiction from J.M. Barrie to Neil Simon*. It was with great pride that I handed him a copy of the manuscript—inscribed as well: "Old friend, dear friend..." More strategic than sincere, I'll admit.

Imagine my astonishment when he returned it to me, accusing me of plagiarism, threatening not only to expose my scholarship as fraudulent but to put a complete stop to my tenure application. As if he knew anything at all about spin-offs from classic mystery fiction!

I did what I had to do.

The triumph? Even if I was convicted of the murder, I was absolved of the stain of plagiarism.

Peer review is a true jury by your peers, and I thank them for it, and the publisher as well for putting the book out despite my circumstances.

Spoofing Suspense remains in print even now, and in many ways its success brings me even more pride than my prison memoir, *Publish, Perish, or Punish: The Dagger in the Library*.

But that one, of course, brought the six-figure advance and the interview in the *New York Times* and the late-night talk show appearances and the royalties still pouring in. True crime confessional, that's where the money is.

So no, please don't call me professor anymore. I no longer want to be part of that world, scrambling for tenure. Bestselling author is the golden ring now, and I've already got that ring in hand.

Mrs. Peacock, with the Candlestick, in the Conservatory

I don't want to talk about that dreadful night in the Boddy mansion. How terribly green Mr. Boddy's tie was. How sweet the Sherry. (Why had I taken that second glass?) I won't discuss those cold, damp corners or the shadows. The skittering in the walls. How large the chunks of meat in the dinner stew were. (I never eat that much, especially not at night.)

Come see all your precious masterpieces on display, he'd told me. Mr. Boddy, my biggest fan. He'd purchased my very first painting, you see. Back when I was showing in back-alley art galleries where they served boxed wine and grocery store cookies at their openings. He'd stayed with me as my career grew. I owed him a visit. I wanted to see my birds, my loves. See if my babies took flight, found their homes, on his mansion walls.

(I'm much better now. If anything, this experience has pushed me to new heights as an artist. Once the trembles stopped, my hands transformed. Created things I never knew I could.)

I'd forgotten to take my pills, you see. My nerves were shot. All those lion statues and hard-edged tables. The sound of breaking glass lured me from my room. The halls were so dark! Dreadful. I had to bring the candle from my room to see, like some sort of hysterical woman out of a gothic movie. I can't think about all those horrid plants in the conservatory, like alien beasts in the darkness. All those windows, becoming mirrors in the dead of night. The flicker of the candlelight that reflected the image of Mr. Boddy standing behind me, moving fast, his hands raised.

Yes, I hit him. Hard. The sound dull and short. How could I forget it? The melted wax splattering on the windows, like a shower of snowflakes.

I've put it all behind me now. I channel my energy into the paintings. My sweet peacocks, brought to life in pigment and oil. In each I paint a small candlestick, hidden somewhere on the canvas, clean and solid with no signs of blood spatter. In each I press a peacock feather, ease it into the paint. (Can you find them?)

Colonel Mustard, with the Revolver, in the Billiard Room

Duty.

In the lexicon of the soldier, the word *duty* stands higher perhaps than all others.

Duty to one's country—this foremost. Duty to one's chosen branch of the armed forces as well, to one's regiment, one's company, one's platoon, one's squad.

Duty as well to your commanding officer—follow orders, at once and without question—but duty also to your fellow soldier. Leave no man behind.

Or woman—let that be emphasized as well.

Chivalry, one might call this latter duty—a soldierly chivalry in my case, part of a code we've sworn to protect. Protect the fairer sex, defend their honor—a loaded word, that one: honor. More precious meaning to that word where the fairer sex is concerned.

Chivalry and honor are old-fashioned words these days, duty as well perhaps. But to a soldier, these are words to live by, or to die by.

Or, indeed, to kill for.

Mr. Boddy—I do not say this lightly—was a man for whom such words had little meaning.

Let me explain that I do not simply abide civilians, do not simply tolerate them. I have, on many occasions, even enjoyed the company of those who've never worn the uniform. They can be amusing companions of a night on leave, and they cannot entirely be blamed for lacking the moral perspective or rigorous diligence of the soldier. In many cases, they've simply not been trained to sharpen such qualities in themselves.

But others…others do not have such qualities to develop in the first place. No latent sense of duty, no dormancy of honor, and in Mr. Boddy's case, chivalry was a completely foreign notion—even basic respect for the weaker sex, for their unblemished purity.

When I happened upon his coarse treatment of Miss Scarlett in the Billiard Room, heard the words he spoke, saw his actions toward her, my sense of duty and, yes, of chivalry compelled me to protect her honor. Fortunately, I always carry my Webley at my side.

Miss Scarlett and I have never discussed what happened—understandably, given the trauma she experienced. Even if she has preferred not to speak at all to me of the incident, I recognize the gratitude she must feel.

But throughout my own ordeal in the aftermath of doing my duty, I thought often of what worse might have happened had I not shown up at such a timely moment. What would Miss Scarlett have done herself? What might any woman want to do in such a moment? And how should we men—we men of honor—help guide women about how to defend their own?

These were the ruminations which led me to develop my seven-week course Col. Mustard's Women Warriors—and if may say so myself, the women who have had the privilege of completing my course emerge from the training with a steely-eyed understanding of the worst that men might do and with a renewed sense of how to counter the cruel attitudes and actions of lesser men, lacking my own high standards.

Miss Scarlett, with the Rope, in the Lounge

I must, my dears, make a living. And no matter what you may think of me, I will continue on.

I cannot help it if Mr. Boddy fell for me. I cannot help it if he found my talents…delightful. If he, like many men before him and after, wanted more. Wanted to scoot right up to the edge and look down, down, down. I cannot help it if he—if we—went a little too far and slipped, fell into the deep darkness.

The lounge, oh the lounge. It was his favorite room to play in. And play is what he always called it, Mr. Boddy, because for him it was a game. A very delicious game.

Mr. Boddy—how his name suited him. For he was a carnal man, all skin and sweat and sighs. A wild one at heart—a man who liked to be tamed. He pushed and pushed, always wanting to go a little further, a little longer, the rope tighter and tighter. The game—oh, what a game it was. Have you ever seen the way nylon can cut? The way just a twist and a tug can break capillaries? Mr. Boddy liked to be breathless—literally—at the moment of release. This is what made him happy.

And I am not a woman who refuses men their happiness.

Afterward, they tried to blame me. They said I was too brutal. They said—some of them, the jealous, petty, ugly ones—that I did it on purpose.

They tried to ruin my name, to shut Scarlett's Study down.

It didn't work, of course. After fifteen years, one gains a certain reputation, a clout. After fifteen years, I've learned from my mistakes. Protected myself. Mr. Boddy signed the contract, just like all my clients did. *At your own risk,* it says. They all know what they are getting into. They *crave* it.

And now? Well, my dears, I am just as successful as ever. In fact, even more so. Men who hear the tale of how Mr. Boddy was found—in the lounge, silk pajama pants at his ankles, a large, satisfying smile on his face—they seek me out. They know I am a woman who will grant their wildest wishes, play their dirtiest games.

Sometimes I do miss the lounge. With its cigar-smoke-saturated curtains and velvet couch, the Oriental rug and the roar, roar, roar of the fireplace. Sometimes I miss the sound of the rope as it tightened. Sometimes I close my eyes and I can almost feel the breath of Mr. Boddy on my cheek, begging for mercy.

But most days, I don't feel a thing.

Mr. Green, in the Dining Room, with the Lead Pipe

Yep. I pounded him thirteen times with a Motion Pro 16" curved tire iron.

They called it a lead pipe in the papers, the stupid pricks too lazy to do any research. Snowflake reporters never changed a tire in their lives. They wouldn't know a spark plug from a wheel bearing.

"He seemed like such a nice guy," my neighbors said about me. The twit in the apartment above me with the noisy bird actually told them about the time I jump-started his Camry like it was a goddamn gift from Jesus Christ himself and not a way to get his oil-leaking piece of shit car out of the visitor's parking spot outside of the building.

Fuck Mr. Boddy and his gray Mercedes GLE Coupe. Fuck the single-spaced typewritten note he'd taped to the inside of his windshield when he brought the car in for an oil and coolant change. The words are burned into my brain. The thought of it even now, years later, makes my blood pressure rise.

"Please do drain the oil in the following way." Step by step, telling *me* how to do *my job.* As if changing the oil wasn't something I could do after chugging a case of Coors Light with one hand duct-taped behind my back. The snobby prick even asked me to take pictures of each step and email them to him.

I did him one better. I brought the pictures to him.

Found him in his dining room. The butler directed me. "Through the foyer, sir. Past the conservatory and down the hall across from the billiard room," he'd said, as if I even knew what that friggin' meant. The maids, the cooks, giving me those looks. Looking at my greasy clothes, big, dirty hands, dark beard, like I was some sort of stain on the mansion.

I'm not kidding—Mr. Boddy was eating off a goddamn silver platter. All alone. Napkin tucked into his crew neck sweater-vest. He'd started to stand, but only got half-way up before I'd strode the length of the table, raised the tire iron…

Here they come. The doctors have arrived. They'll give me my medicine now. It helps me forget, they say, but I'll never forget. I may sleep, but I'll never forget. There are some things you never forget. The first cigarette, behind the shed. The first engine you rebuild from scratch. The way rubber smells on hot pavement. Those blue and red lights, bouncing off the chandelier above Mr. Boddy's dining room table.

And I'll never forget Mr. Boddy's signature, there on the bottom of that single-spaced typed note. *I'm sure you won't get it wrong! You're the best! Mr. B.*

I drained his plug alright. Watched all the liquid pool out.

Nope, that I'll never forget.

Mrs. White, with the Wrench, in the Study

I was born into the Boddy family. Or adjacent to it at least. That latter distinction was stressed to me at a young age.

My mother had been little more than a teenager herself when she first entered service to the Boddy family, and I'm certain she appreciated the security of the position, especially later, as a single mother, assured of a place for her child to live and food on the table for one more hungry mouth. Me.

What was provision for her seemed extravagance to me. As a very young child, you don't recognize such things as class distinctions and hierarchy, and for much of that childhood, I actually thought of the house as no less my own than anyone else's who lived there. Obviously, my mother dressed differently than the Boddy family, in her black dress and white apron same as the other servants, but—call me ignorant—I don't remember understanding then what that meant, especially when Bertram was my age and my playmate and seemingly my equal.

Bertram. That was his name, so it was what I called him then. Bert, in fact. In different ways over the years, *Bertram* felt uncomfortable on my tongue.

I still remember clearly the morning when Bertram's mother heard me calling for him in the hallway—"Bert! Bert!" I was eight at the time, eager to find my best friend, eager to play. His mother stopped me and stooped down and stroked my hair back and told me I should have better manners, told me I should be old enough to recognize that it wasn't proper for me to call him by his Christian name.

"From now on, you are to refer to my son as Master Boddy, do you understand?" And from the way her fingernails grazed my forehead and that look in her eye and the tone of her voice, suddenly I did.

Master Boddy he became, and then Mr. Boddy.

Gradually, he recognized the change himself. I don't know if his mother had explained to him, too, the difference between his place and mine, but soon the Bertram I knew—my best friend—was gone. Our relationship changed, and continued to change, always in confusing ways. A hurtful distance as I seemed simply to disappear from his view. A burning humiliation when I joined the staff and he began to issue orders my way, luxuriating in his power over me. Then a deeper confusion when he asserted that power in more… personal ways.

For a short while, I believed that our childhood friendship might have rekindled itself as love, that both our old ties and now this new…affection between us might bridge those differences, that I might become—in actuality—part of the Boddy family.

But that was, as I said, only for a short while.

You become accustomed to the duties. You become accustomed to the hierarchy. You become accustomed to your place. And you're busy, of course. The rugs need vacuuming, the furniture needs dusting, the door needs answering, the mail needs sorting, the silverware needs polishing, the toilets need scrubbing—or repairing. So many small repairs here and there. You take initiative if you want to keep your position. I became as handy with a pair of pliers as with my polishing rag.

In time, I married. Mr. White was a butler to the Boddy family. A gentle man, older than me, unfortunately already in fading health. He wanted children, and though I failed to give those to him, we remained fond of one another. It was a more than adequate marriage for someone such as me. Even today, I miss so terribly his warmth and kindness.

When Mr. White passed, I submerged myself more fully in my duties for the Boddy family, Bertram now at its head, and ultimately rose to supervise the domestic staff—and then the entire staff, not only the butler and the maids but the cooks in the kitchen, the landscapers, the maintenance men, everyone. Head of house. Hiring and directing and checking behind and calling up short and ultimately responsible for overseeing every detail.

Seeing those necessary details—and ignoring the ones I was expected *not* to see. Not only Mr. Boddy's indiscretions with the many women in his own social circle, even the married ones, but also his lingering gaze at some fresh maid or serving girl, his untoward advances in those directions, the lines crossed and then recrossed, and that same look again and again in each young woman's eye, a cascade of feelings and emotions.

Shame.

Hope.

Disbelief.

You now? You next? I knew the look well, having lived it.

None of those women discussed their situations with me. Likely none of them felt they could dare. Still, I had trusted that they felt my empathy somehow, some spirit of the sisterhood of women, some glimpse in my eyes of understanding about what we had all endured.

But over time, I saw no reflection of sisterhood in return from those women, no recognition at all. Instead, I saw myself through their eyes: not merely an older woman now, but an old one. At their age, you simply don't think that we've known what you know, been where you are. You hardly see us at all.

Call me ignorant again. Only too late did I recognize something else: that I had fallen into that same blind spot myself in my own younger days.

Only then did I return my thinking to my own mother, little more than a teenager herself when she first entered service to the Boddy family. Only then did I wonder more about my father, the one I had asked about and asked about and got no answer.

Only then did I remember a fresh detail about that morning when Bertram's mother instructed me to call her son "Master." Her husband had been standing with her, behind her, looking down on me. I hadn't remembered him there because he had never said a word.

The elder Mr. Boddy was, of course, long deceased. But the iniquities of the fathers, as they say, are visited on the sons, and perhaps the responsibilities for atoning those sins as well.

The authorities got it wrong in the end. I don't know who hit my Bertram—I will say his name now, my equal, no doubt—with that wrench in the study. Any number of people could likely have killed him, had reason to. But yes, my fingerprints were on the weapon. My fingerprints were everywhere in that house: silverware, decorations, cabinets, furniture, toiletries, tools, everywhere.

In the end, though, what does the tool matter? Or who swung it?

Even without the wrench, he would've died that night.

Mrs. White, with the poison, in her pantry.

No one had *that* combination in mind.

⚔

Art Taylor (arttaylorwriter.com) is the author of two collections: *The Adventure of the Castle Thief and Other Expeditions and Indiscretions* and *The Boy Detective & The Summer of '74 and Other Tales of Suspense*. His work has won the Edgar, Agatha, Anthony, Derringer, and Macavity Awards. He is an associate professor of English at George Mason University.

Tara Laskowski is the author of the suspense novels *The Weekend Retreat*, *The Mother Next Door*, and *One Night Gone*, which won the Agatha Award, Macavity Award, and the Anthony Award. She has won the Agatha Award and Thriller Award for her short fiction and was the longtime editor of the online flash fiction journal *SmokeLong Quarterly*.

PROMISES TO KEEP

GERT-JAN VAN DEN BEMD

TRANSLATED FROM THE DUTCH BY JOSH PACHTER

"What can I do for you, young lady?"

The voice that comes from the little speaker above the four doorbells anonymously labeled 4A, 4B, 4C, and 4D is soft, overly formal. Apparently, its owner can see me, though I don't spot a camera in the small foyer between the unlocked street door and the locked inner door, a checkerboard of alternating clear and frosted panes of glass.

"I'm here about the—"

"Ah, Mrs. van Tilt, I'll be right down."

A moment later, a silhouette appears behind the glass, and the door swings open. The man reminds me of the farmer in that famous American painting, not just because of his white shirt and black suit jacket but also thanks to his high domed forehead and wire-rimmed spectacles and close-cropped gray hair.

"The buzzer that unlocks the door is broken," he explains.

He leads me up a flight of granite steps. His apartment door stands open. His slippers whisper across the hallway's laminate floor, my sneakers squeak with every step. He shows me into a compact living room. The ceiling, the wooden paneling, the floor, the furniture, everything is in shades of brown. One lonely photograph hangs on the wall: a man and a woman in Seventies hairstyles standing before a white wooden house. More "American Gothic." No, that's not true. These two are better looking than the farm couple.

"Sit down, please, and I'll go and get it."

He nods at a caramel-colored love seat. The cracked leather pillows at each end might have been left out in the sun for years. There are no plants in the room. A glass vase on an end table is lined with lime rings suggestive of long-ago bouquets.

The man comes back with a cardboard shoebox. I can read the label: black pumps, size thirty-six. He sits opposite me in an armchair exactly the right size to hold him, as if it has been molded to the precise measurements of his body.

He deposits the box on a low coffee table and lifts the lid. "Here it is," he says solemnly, "the 1139."

We look down at a model locomotive, lovingly built of gray and yellow plastic and lying like a dead wagtail on a bed of shredded crinkle-cut packing paper.

The man waits patiently for my reaction, but for a moment I'm at a loss for words.

"What did we say?" he finally asks. "Fifty Euros?"

I clear my throat. "Yes," I say, "but—"

"But?"

"But what about the other item?"

"The other item?" He glances at the locomotive. "There's just the 1139. Everything else is gone." His smile turns melancholic, and I realize that the train car is perhaps the last remaining piece of what has been for him a beloved hobby.

"I mean the gun."

"Excuse me?"

"The gun. The Luger."

The smile vanishes from his face. "I don't know what you're talking about."

"Your other ad. It was only online for a moment, but I happened to see it. Someone must have reported it to the webmaster, and they deleted it. I suppose selling firearms over the internet isn't permitted."

The man looks at me, and I can't tell if his confusion is real or feigned. "I don't have a gun," he says. "I've never had a gun."

I force an understanding smile. "You don't have to worry, I'm not a police officer. I want to buy the Luger. The ad said one hundred Euros."

He gets to his feet. Without a word, he fits the lid back onto the shoebox and leaves the room. I can hear him rummaging around in what I assume must be a spare room used for storage. An ironing board, a mountain of laundry, a toolbox, cartons of accumulated knickknacks, piles of yellowing newspapers and magazines. Somewhere amidst all of that is another cardboard box, or perhaps he has it wrapped in a square of canvas. I can almost smell it, oil and metal. *Let's go,* I think. *You want to be rid of it.*

The man returns. His hands are empty.

"A hundred and fifty for the gun," I say, but he walks past me in silence and opens the door to the entry hall.

"Good evening, Mrs. van Tilt," he says, turning my name into an insult.

He doesn't accompany me down the hall to the apartment door. The lock is tricky, and he brushes past me with a sigh. I smell soap and something woodsy. I step back to give him room, but now I'm further inside the apartment than he is, which stirs a feeling of discomfort.

Behind me, someone coughs.

A woman—dyed blond hair, eyeglasses with pink lenses—is looking at me. In her hands is a small carton, smaller than the shoebox.

"Come with me," she says.

The man swallows an oath and relocks the apartment door.

* * * *

The woman and I sit side by side on the love seat. The man remains standing. The little box is on the coffee table, its lid removed. Inside is a Pistole Parabellum P08, commonly referred to by the last name of its designer, Georg Luger.

"He promised me." She nods at the photograph on the wall. "That was taken on the day of our engagement, forty-three years ago. We promised each other that, if one of us ever wanted to die, the other would arrange it. We bought that thing"—she waves a hand at the gun—"and agreed that it was what we would use. Pills are so uncertain. And now I'm ready, but he turns out to be a coward."

The man closes his eyes.

"Six years ago," his wife says, "I was diagnosed with cancer. They had to remove my left breast. They took the right one, too, although it was perfectly healthy. 'Just to be safe,' the doctor said. *Safe*."

She rests her small right hand for a moment on the curve of her knitted sweater. "He offered to 'recreate my femininity,' was how he put it, and he gave me a choice between silicone or saline implants. I was so thin he couldn't use my own tissue for the reconstruction. Thin as a rail, even then." She laughs ruefully. "I chose silicone because I thought it looked more natural. Within a year, one of them began to leak. They had to remove it, but it was too late: the poison had already spread through my body. It infiltrated my nervous system. Sometimes the pain is absolutely unbearable."

"Would you like something to drink?" the man says, but the offer comes across as a diversionary tactic, an attempt to distract his wife from her story. "Coffee? Tea?"

"I've known for a week now that it's time." She taps an index finger against the side of her head. "It's here, now, too. I can't go on any longer, it's more than I can live with. Can you understand that?"

I nod.

"But he won't do it."

"I love her too much," the man says hoarsely.

"Nonsense! You loved me more when you made your promise than you love me now. When we were in bed, you kissed my feet, you touched me in places you won't even *look* at now. I repulse you."

"That's not *true*, Kathy. I love you as much as I ever did. It's just...I couldn't go on without you."

"If you don't do what you promised, Yves, that won't keep me with you.

It'll only make the loss harder and sadder."

She reaches into the box and grabs the pistol by its barrel. "Here! Do it!"

I jump up and stand between the man and the gun, my thigh brushing for a moment against the black metal.

"Was it you who advertised the gun for sale?" I ask the woman.

She nods hopelessly, her anger spent, and lays the pistol on her lap.

"I hoped someone without such high moral standards might see it and come." A smile flickers across her face. "Perhaps a professional. *I* would have paid *him*—I have some money saved." She raised her chin to indicate her husband. "He saw the ad and deleted it. But not before *you* saw it, and connected it with the other one he'd placed, the one for his bloody trains."

"I'm not the professional you hoped for."

"You can't always get what you want," she says wryly.

For a full minute, the three of us stare wordlessly at the gun.

How soundproof is this room, I wonder. All I can hear is the woman's slow breathing, which synchronizes with her index finger as it strokes the Luger's dull barrel.

"We'll do it together, you and me," I tell her husband, and then add to Kathy, "if that's all right with you."

She nods. "Oh, yes," she says, and turns to him. "It's what I want, Yves. Please."

He looks at me, ashamed of his weakness, grateful for my courage.

"I'll get everything ready," he says.

* * * *

Kathy lies on top of the comforter that decorates their double bed. She's freshened her makeup, brushed her hair, put on a hint of perfume, changed into a black dress, nylons, and pumps, as if she's off to a party. Her husband has put on a tie and patent leather shoes. I feel like a slob in my T-shirt and jeans.

Yves sits on his side of the bed. The surface of the nightstand beside him is bare, except for a simple lamp. The matching nightstand on her side, where I'm sitting, is littered with blister packs and plastic bottles of medications and painkillers.

He hands her a square pillow embroidered with the image of a sad-eyed faun.

"Should I give you two some privacy?" I ask—but I know that, if I leave the bedroom, I'll never find the nerve to return.

"No, stay," she says. "You're part of the family now."

The man nods his agreement. He leans down and kisses her on the lips, then on the forehead. He gently moves her hands so the pillow is against the side of her head.

"Not there," she says, and lays the pillow on her chest.

I pick up the Luger. Despite its slim shape, it's heavy in my hand, much heavier than I would have expected, as if all the mass in the room has drained into it, and the bed, the nightstands, the three of us have become weightless.

I touch the end of the barrel to the pillow, right between the faun's sad eyes. Yves's hand is rough and hot. Mine encircles the grip, but I leave room for his finger on the trigger, and then Kathy's hands wrap around ours, her palms and fingers in the shape of a heart. Now only the barrel remains visible, a little black finger pointing at the woman lying on the bed.

She looks at me—in politeness or gratitude, I don't know which—but I will her to turn away, back to her husband, where her gaze belongs. He kisses her again, and for a moment lays his head against her bottle-blond hair.

She whispers something in his ear and closes her eyes.

The pillow muffles the report, and a lone feather floats into the air.

* * * *

We descend the granite steps together and reach for the lobby door at the same time. Our fingers touch. His flesh is cold, now, even colder than mine.

"You'll be okay?" I ask.

"Yes," he says. "I'll tell the police I heard a shot, and went in and found her dead."

"They'll suspect you. They always suspect the spouse."

"I'll be fine," he assures me. "Whatever happens."

He makes a half-hearted attempt to hug me and opens the door. Despite the warmth of the evening, a chill runs down my spine.

"You don't have to answer this," he says, nodding at the cardboard shoe-box in my hands. "You told me you wanted the locomotive for your husband. Did you want the gun for him, too?"

"No," I say, "the gun was for me. I thought my life had lost its meaning. I was wrong."

I step out into the moonlight, and, smiling, he swings the door shut behind me.

✗

Gert-Jan van den Bemd is a Dutch writer and artist. He holds a PhD in Endocrinology from Erasmus University Rotterdam and a bachelor's degree in art from Sint Joost School of Art & Design in Breda/'s-Hertogenbosch in The Netherlands. He likes to wander around, especially in New York, Normandy (France), and Ostend (Belgium).

Josh Pachter is an author, editor, and translator of crime fiction.

A COLD DAY IN HELENA

JOHN M. FLOYD

"Are we sure we want to do this?" Ray asked.

Will Hardy, a man of few words anyway, didn't reply. Instead, he sat with both hands on the wheel and stared through the windshield at the front courtyard of First National Bank. He and Ray were parked at the curb just up the street from the bank, not too close and not too far away.

"I said—"

"I heard you." Will turned to look at his younger brother. "You got another solution?"

He didn't bother to list all the problems that needed solutions. Overdue mortgage payment on their shared farmhouse, leaky roof, cutoff threats from the water and power companies, a twenty-year-old pickup truck that had to decide every morning whether it would start. And on top of all that, he and Ray were both out of work. Not that it was a great loss of income— the Hardy brothers had been, until last Friday, after-hours broompushers at the local canning plant.

"There are other jobs," Ray said, reading his mind.

Will faced front again and studied the bank. "You know of any, off-hand?"

"There must be. What would you want, if you had your pick?"

"Other than tennis pro at the country club?"

"Other than that."

Will thought it over. "Security guard," he said. "I did that, once."

"You're kidding."

"Nope. Didn't last long. You were up in Atlanta then, with Yvonne." Both brothers were long since divorced, having chosen brides as poorly as they'd chosen livelihoods. "I liked it. Good hours, good pay, no manual labor, nice uniform."

"Plus, you got to carry your gun around," Ray said. Will loved his guns. Sniper in Iraq, trick-shot artist at the county fair, two-time winner of the state Turkey Shoot.

Will shrugged. "Water under the bridge. Nobody'd hire me for that now, nor you neither. Security guys don't have long hair *or* long rap sheets. Even if the list is mostly misdemeanors."

They both fell silent. Overhead, the sky was gray as a tombstone, and snow was in the forecast. Again, Will checked his watch.

"I'm freezing in here," Ray said. "How much longer?"

"Fifteen minutes." Will hadn't explained his timetable, but all the reading he'd done said Tuesday mornings were a bank's slowest time of the week. Best of all was ten-thirty, exactly halfway between opening and noon. And he figured they needed every advantage they could get. After another silence Ray said, "Nobody'll get hurt, on this. Right?"

"That's the plan."

"Then why are we carrying guns?"

Will gave him a look. "So the bank folks'll do what they're told. They need to see 'em."

Ray seemed to ponder that. "Does yours have bullets in it?"

"What? Sure it does."

"Why, if you're not gonna use it?"

Will shut his eyes and let out a breath. "Tell you what. Unload yours, if you want to. If I see I have to shoot anybody, I'll shoot 'em in the leg."

"Better yet, use a straw and a spitball," Ray said.

They looked at each other and grinned. "Or make a face at 'em?" Will said.

"Or employ strong language."

They laughed aloud. Will thought it was the first time he'd smiled in a week.

The lighthearted mood didn't last. Ray kept shivering and Will kept watching. He'd seen no customers entering or leaving for the past ten minutes. So far so good.

Don't kid yourself, Will thought. This wouldn't be easy. Even the weather had him worried. Snow in Florida? That couldn't be a good sign.

But the plan itself was sound. Stroll down to the bank, pull their masks on at the front door, have the tellers fill two cloth bags with money, exit through the rear door to the alley, and dash down the back steps of the Helena County courthouse next door, where they would wait in an empty and forgotten storage closet until the excitement blew over. After a reasonable time, an hour maybe, they would replace their zippered jackets and masks with two old trenchcoats and baseball caps that Will had stored in the closet and leave with the money stuffed into the baggy pockets of their long coats. Within fifteen minutes they'd be able to circle around and approach their parked pickup from the other side, and—if the damn thing would crank—make a delayed but clean getaway. Then they could celebrate, patch their roof, fix their truck, pay their bills. Maybe even take a little break before trying to find new jobs. One solution at a time.

"What do you think?" Ray asked, after another wait.

"You got your mask?"

"In my pocket. With the empty bag."

"It's ten twenty-five," Will said. "Let's go."

* * * *

The streets and sidewalks were almost deserted, typical for a cold, gloomy morning in a southern town. This wasn't New England, or Michigan, or Montana. This was January in the Florida Panhandle. Folks who didn't have to be out and about were inside their cozy homes and offices, talking or working or dreaming of springtime.

The Hardy brothers' truck was parked fifty yards south of the bank, on the opposite side of Panama Street. They stepped out onto the sidewalk, their breaths smoking in the frigid air, and saw two young women in long fleece coats come out of a coffeeshop just past the bank and head toward them. Snowflakes were falling quietly from the slate-gray sky. Deep in conversation, the two women approached the bank on its side of the street while Will and Ray started toward it on the other. And just as the young women reached the courtyard surrounding the entrance—

Shots rang out from inside the bank building—automatic-weapons fire, Will thought, remembering the Army—and two people in black hoodies burst through the front door and hurried toward the street. Both held bulging gym bags and assault rifles. Behind them, a voice shouted, "Stop 'em!" and one of the pair turned and fired at the doorway, *powpowpowpow*. Then, after a moment of dead silence, three things happened in quick succession: (1) the two women froze in their tracks, clapped their mittened hands to their hearts, and let out ear-piercing screams; (2) the black-clad robbers, clearly shaken now, whirled together toward the new noise and raised their weapons; and (3) Will Hardy pulled a longbarreled .38 revolver from his waistband and shot them both.

Will stood motionless, his smoking pistol still aimed and steady. He was vaguely aware that the two young women were staring wide-eyed at him, and that Ray had sprinted the forty yards to the scene and was standing over the wounded suspects, kicking their weapons away and covering them with his own revolver. Scattered on the cold paving stones were dozens of banded greenish-white packets of cash spilled from one of the unzipped gym bags. His heart pounding, Will lowered his gun and let out a lungful of air before trudging forward to join his brother.

So far no one else had dared to poke his head out of the bank. While Ray kept a careful watch on the two moaning robbers, Will knelt beside them—one, he saw for the first time, was a woman—and frisked them both. Surprisingly, they had no other weapons. He was reaching for his phone to call 911 when he heard distant sirens and realized someone inside, or maybe one of the young women, must've already raised the alarm. The excitement was over.

He looked at Ray and sighed. So much for their plan.

* * * *

By noon the courtyard looked almost normal again, except for a coating of white. So did the street. The emergency vehicles, news vans, and most of the police cars were gone now, along with the pair of young ladies, the wounded prisoners, the dead bodies of two bank employees, and a legion of curious and gawking townsfolk. Will and Ray Hardy stood together just inside the entrance to the bank, sipping from Styrofoam cups of coffee and watching the snow and waiting for Officer Edward Nesbit of the Helena PD, who had asked them to hang around awhile. They'd already been interviewed, congratulated, questioned, and inspected by more people than Will had seen in one place in years. Most of the faces were familiar, some were not. Several patrolmen had driven up from Pensacola. Will had noticed, before coming inside, that most of the blood on the paving stones was hidden under the dusting of snow.

Finally, Nesbit joined them, his face grim. "Crazy day," he said. "First bank robbery I can remember, in this town, and the first snowfall since I was a teenager." He paused and looked them in the eye. He and Will went way back, and not all the times had been good. "The Hardy Boys to the rescue," he said.

"We need to get going, Eddie," Will said. "We done, here?"

"Almost. Just a few more things." Nesbit dug a notepad from his pocket, checked one of the pages. "You said you were both in your truck, just down the street, when you saw the two suspects come out of the bank. Correct?"

"Yep. And heard the shots."

"That's when you grabbed your guns and came to help."

"Right. Mine was under my seat, Ray's was in the glovebox. They're legal, we got permits."

"And then you heard the women scream," Nesbit said, reading from his notes, "and saw the suspects turn and point their weapons at them."

"They were gonna kill 'em, Eddie. I could see that, even from that far away."

Nesbit nodded. "Both women agree. They say you saved their lives."

"The timing was lucky," Will said.

"Those two shots of yours," Nesbit said. "That was a long way off, for a handgun."

"Didn't have much choice in the matter."

"No, I don't guess you did." A silence passed, while Nesbit studied the notepad. "The only thing is…one of the ladies says she thought she noticed you and Ray already out of your vehicle and walking, before the suspects exited the bank."

"What'd the other lady say?"

"She agrees with your version. Never saw you until you fired your gun."

Will glanced at Ray, then looked at Nesbit and shrugged. "The first woman was mistaken."

Again, Nesbit nodded, slowly. "Must've been. Otherwise, you and Ray would've already been walking toward the bank with guns in your pockets. And why would you be doing that?"

"We wouldn't."

"No, I guess not. One more thing: Why *were* you here, today? Why'd you come?"

"To get a check cashed," Will said.

"And with all the excitement, you never got a chance to do that, I suppose."

"No. I didn't."

"Can I see the check?"

For a long moment the two of them stared at each other. Then Will took out his wallet, removed a folded check, and handed it to Nesbit.

"Ray cashed his yesterday," Will said. "Our last payments from the canning plant."

Another nod. "I heard they let some folks go, the other day. Bad luck."

"Hope you'll let us know, you hear about any job openings," Ray said.

"Might not have to." Nesbit handed the check back to Will. "Mr. Dewberry told me to give you a message for him."

Will frowned. "The bank president? What's he want with me?"

"He wants to hire you. Both of you."

The Hardys exchanged a puzzled look.

"What?" Ray said.

"Don't look so surprised. You boys stopped a robbery in progress, caught the two thieves—who are also murderers—and recovered the stolen money. Not a bad day's work."

Will narrowed his eyes. "Eddie, we don't know anything about banking. Neither of us."

"I don't think it matters."

"Why not? What's the job?"

"Security guards."

Will swallowed. "You serious?"

"Yep. At three times what they been paying you at the plant."

"How does Dewberry know how much they paid us?"

"Don't matter. He's tripling it. Said he needs your answer by the end of the week."

A silence passed. Will finally said, "Something's funny here. What are you not telling us?"

Nesbit stayed quiet another few seconds. "One a them two ladies that almost got shot?"

"What about her?"

"She's Dewberry's niece." Nesbit stood up and said, "You fellas done a good thing, here today." Then he turned to leave—and stopped.

Dazed, Will said, "There's more?"

"Only one question. Those two robbers. How is it you shot 'em both in the leg?"

Will shrugged. "Just worked out that way."

The two of them studied each other another moment, then Nesbit nodded and left. He crossed the courtyard, pulling up his collar against the snow, and climbed into his cruiser. The brothers watched him until he was out of sight.

"All this slow-time-at-the-bank research I did," Will thought aloud. "I wish we'd got here ten minutes earlier."

"What?" Ray said.

"Maybe nobody would've died."

They were both quiet, looking out the window. Sipping their coffee.

"What if we'd got here ten minutes later?" Ray asked.

It was a good point.

* * * *

Back in their truck, on their way home, Ray said, "What do you think?"

"About the job offer?" Will had been thinking of nothing else. He scratched his two-day beard, watching the road. The snow had lightened up a bit. "I think you might have to keep your gun loaded, from now on."

Ray grinned. "And get a haircut?"

"Heaven forbid," Will said.

He slowed down and crept across the bridge at the edge of town. It looked icy. He wondered how people drove in this stuff. When they were back up to speed, he fished around in his pocket and pulled out his mask. "Here—take this damn thing and burn it. Yours too. We're lucky they didn't search us."

Ray tucked both masks into a paper sack. After a pause he said, "Speaking of which—"

"Yeah?"

"That paycheck in your wallet. I thought you cashed that at the store yesterday, like I did."

"I decided to hold onto it awhile. Just in case."

They let several miles go past, saying nothing. Finally, Will glanced at his brother's profile. Ray was never quiet. "What is it?"

Ray took something from his own pocket, held it up. A thick, bound packet of hundred-dollar bills. Will almost ran off the road.

"I decided to hold onto this, too," Ray said.

Now they were both grinning. Maybe they *would* be able to catch up on the bills soon, Will thought, and repairs too. And working at three times their former pay…

He felt his smile widen. Maybe snow on the Gulf Coast wasn't a bad omen after all.

"Wonder if they'll give us uniforms," he said.

John M. Floyd is the author of more than a thousand short stories in publications like *Alfred Hitchcock's Mystery Magazine, Ellery Queen's Mystery Magazine, Strand Magazine, The Saturday Evening Post, Best American Mystery Stories,* and *Best Mystery Stories of the Year.* A former Air Force captain and IBM systems engineer, John is an Edgar Award finalist, a Shamus Award winner, a five-time Derringer Award winner, and the author of seven collections of short mystery fiction. He is also the 2018 recipient of the Edward D. Hoch Memorial Golden Derringer for lifetime achievement.

HUMAN WASTE

DAVIN IRELAND

The barrels arrive at all hours of the day and night. Blue, black, yellow sometimes—I couldn't tell you where they're from. All I do is process the contents and make sure the empty is waiting for collection on the return trip. A parade of sullen drivers only adds to the mystery. Most of them don't even speak English. The colossal delivery trucks materialize from the pulsating heat-shimmer out on US 95, titanic bulks hurtling south to north, Idaho their rumored destination. Then they're gone again. This derelict gas station is their only stop in Arizona.

The cartel never uses young men. Their latest emissary is a middle-aged Latino with a sagging paunch and a fondness for plaid shirts. No matter which one he wears, the sleeves are always rolled up to just above the elbow, as if this place were a blood bank and he a willing donor. Salt-and-pepper hair curls from beneath his faded baseball cap. He never communicates in words if an informed grunt will suffice. His expression remains eternally fixed—wind-burned features a mask that forms part of a broader, impenetrable façade. He visited here three times in a week once. Previously we'd taken no deliveries for a year.

So, the driver. He disclosed his name this one time, inadvertently. His cell phone buzzed while he was getting a soda from the machine. He answered with a curt, *Jorge*. Just one word: no greeting or question necessary. I guess his manner fits our surroundings, which are spare, cheerless, and neglected. We have gas pumps but no gas. We process hazardous waste without a license. Passing motorists rarely mistake this place for a viable business. When they do, the forfeit is pitiless and unrelenting. I should know: I was one of those people once. Fleeing across the state line in an effort to avoid a felony charge, I took a wrong turn and that was that. I've been here ever since, just another a drifter entombed in the vaults of the shadow economy.

Today is no different. Today is Sunday and there's work to be done. Newly-arrived, Jorge's giant truck dominates the concrete forecourt, engine dead but radiating insufferable heat. With my head pounding and the stench of diesel fumes rank in my nostrils, I mentally prepare for the ordeal to come. Jorge descends wordlessly from the cab, the soles of his shoes worn through to the linings, and raises his chin at me. I tilt my chin to the appropriate angle in response. That's as close to a formal greeting as we'll get. Ritual complete, we make our way to the rear of the truck. Soon I'm ploughing through huddles of empty petroleum barrels and yellow carbon-steel salvage drums marked with chemical waste decals.

There's only one white barrel in here. It's brimming, plastered with grimy contact smudges, and marked out by a single yellow-and-black *CORROSIVE* sticker. We drag it out onto the tail-lift, contents slopping noisily against the inner walls. It's as if whatever's inside is trying to get out. A warehouse trolley awaits. I wheel the barrel into the main building. Strap on a breathing mask. Pop the lid. For a moment, neither of us moves. The thin scum floating on the surface of the plum-colored liquid within has congealed. The sludge at the bottom of the barrel, when I get that far, will retain the consistency of jellied beef stock and be as black as crude oil. It's this rancid base layer that conceals the trinkets. I can't bring myself to think of them as trophies.

Flesh and bone do not survive submersion in hydrofluoric acid. Fabrics fare no better. If you're familiar with that TV show everybody raved about, you'll know why. You may also recall that some materials are impervious to that particular form of corrosion. Example. I once dredged a nickel-plated belt buckle out of a barrel that had come all the way from Oaxaca City. It was in perfect condition, gleaming like a coin retrieved from a fountain on a summer's day. I still wear it when the mood takes me. From another came a plastic photocard driving license. Also, if the victim is over thirty-five, it's not unusual to recover little flecks of the silver-mercury amalgam used in old-fashioned dental fillings. I sift the sludge for those tiny glinting specks as carefully as a prospector panning for gold and am equally thrilled when they come to light. Further acquisitions include a pair of silver stud earrings and a white gold wedding ring, all from the same barrel. Whoever performed the disposal that day must have been in a hurry. Oversights of that nature mean I've amassed a collection numbering about two-dozen items at last count. I keep my souvenirs in an old cedar-wood cigar box. I am in the habit of poring over them before turning in for the night. This is more than just my way of honoring the dead. These relics of lost humanity are the closest thing to friends I am ever likely to have.

* * * *

Jorge is waiting for me when I shuffle back into the glare of the noonday sun. The heat is merciless at this time of the year. Not that my guest seems to notice. Or maybe he doesn't care. He says, "The last barrel was marked," and snaps the top on his customary soda.

"Marked?"

"Outside. The base. Trace organic matter."

I mentally flash on the hitchhiker who turned up at the plant around the time of the last collection. Young, skinny, sporting a three-day growth of beard and an infuriatingly easy manner, he ambled along with a rucksack slung over one shoulder and smiled indulgently when he saw me. "Name's Lincoln Gower," he drawled, stale marijuana flavoring his breath. "Was hoping to use the rest room?"

He'd toured the whole site on his own by the time our paths crossed, and in so doing had sealed his fate. We tracked down the dozing security guard and the three of us smoked a blunt together. Spent most of the afternoon playing cards and debating the bewildering decline of baseball. I thought I'd convinced Lincoln to stay. I was wrong about that. Toward sundown he just packed up his stuff and said it was time to hit the road. Such a terrible waste. I must have dragged that empty barrel through a stray smear of whatever he left behind. Sometimes that mop gets so damn bloody, all it does is distribute the DNA over a wider area (not unlike the drivers, if you think about it). The problem is, thinking about it makes me sad. I look at the ground and mutter, "It won't happen again."

Jorge, however, is far from satisfied. He kicks the latest empty, which stands on the baking concrete forecourt like an unfulfilled threat, and squints at me. Sweat squeezes from the wrinkles at the corners of his eyes. "You clean this one too?"

"Twice." The lie comes naturally.

He sips from the can. Does it thoughtfully. The taste of the soda seems to figure in his thinking. He smacks his lips, wipes them on the coarse hairs of his forearm. Those rolled-up sleeves again. "What did you use?"

"Industrial detergent, scrubbed it inside and out."

Another sip, followed by a perfunctory belch. "Did you hose it down or sluice it out with buckets of well-water?"

"Pressure-washed it, same as always."

Jorge chugs the remainder of his drink, tosses the empty can at me. It hits me in the chest, clatters to the ground. "The cartel won't permit another mistake," he divulges. "You're lucky I caught this one when I did."

There's nothing more to say. I double-check the cleaned barrel because it is expected of me, and load it by hand. The rear doors clang shut. The engine bellows like a wounded mastodon. The last I see of Jorge, I'm standing on the shoulder of the highway, the towering delivery truck rippling away into the heat shimmer of northern Arizona. It dissolves every bit as easily as the bodies of the condemned dissolve in that greedy acid. Something tells me I won't be around to process the next shipment.

* * * *

Night falls. The moon rides high in the cloudless sky over Yuma County. It's bitterly cold out. My ascent into the hills flanking US 95 begins at the mouth of an old wash littered with broken rocks. The ironwoods flanking the wash's alkaline course are crowned with gorgeous reddish-purple flowers that smell of nothing. Night-blooming cacti huddle beneath their spread. The darkness welcomes me with its conspiracy of silence.

The climb is treacherous, but worth the endeavor. The ravine on the other side of the summit is the deepest I know. I seek out a rock worn smooth by previous generations of visitors and take a seat. Peer into the darkness below. My friends are heaped together in the narrow channel of the dry riverbed down there. My own work, not the cartel's. The bare bones, whitened further by an abundance of lunar light, have been picked clean by the coyotes and the vultures. I commune with them when I can, articulate all the thoughts and feelings I would have shared had their owners proven compassionate enough to spare me a day or two of their time.

Just a day or two. Is that too much to ask?

Lincoln Gower thought it was.

Heart encumbered with regret, I take out the cigar box and empty it into the ravine. The contents drop, tumble, see-saw toward the depths in a discreet flutter. I relax my grip on the box, and it sinks out of sight like a fading memory.

I get to my feet, tighten the straps on Lincoln's canvas knapsack. His boots are a little narrow for my feet, but his clothes fit me perfectly now that I have achieved my fasting weight. The stubble on my cheeks itches as it lengthens into a scrubby beard. The face that stares out of the mirror each morning bears an uncanny resemblance to the one on the dead man's driving license. I'm all set. No sign of the cartel these last three weeks, which means no more hiding and no more death. Just a young man with a new identity, the open road ahead of him, and a whole lot to make up for.

Maybe not such a waste after all.

✗

Davin Ireland's fiction credits include stories published in more than ninety print magazines and anthologies around the world, including *Grift, Underworlds, Mystery Magazine, The Horror Express, Mystery Tribune, Pseudopod, Storyteller Magazine,* and *Something Wicked,* as well as selected digital markets. You can visit his site at davinireland.com.

HIVA-OA

J.W. WOOD

for Rocco

They found Janine's body a week before I was due to return to the States. She'd been bludgeoned and left to die in a ravine half a mile outside Atuona. As usual, I had a terrible hang-over when I found out. What else was there to do on a tiny island except drink yourself into oblivion?

Janine was married to the local Baptist missionary, Ian McLellan. They'd been on Hiva-Oa for two years. I'd met them through the cocktail-party circuit: fifteen ex-pat couples and the odd single aid worker traipsing round each other's houses for damp martinis and wilting *amuse-bouches.* The French government's local representative held the best parties—he represented *la République,* after all, and had an entertainment budget to match his status.

"Michael, is it?"

When I met her at the Governor's *soirée,* she wore a little black dress edged with lace, cut low at the front. She was early thirties, pale skin and black hair brushed to shoulder length. She was American—beyond that I couldn't place her accent.

"So how are you liking this real-life production of *South Pacific?*" she smiled, running a neat fingernail round her empty glass.

"I love it. I'm with the Peace Corps—"

"The Peace Corps? Oh, how—Ian, darling! Have you met Michael, the new guy? Michael, meet my husband, Ian."

I shook Ian's hand. His grip was clammy, like the man himself. Lanky, bespectacled, and unsmiling—every inch the unbending moralist. I felt barely controlled anger, even at that first meeting. For all that she was alluring, he talked like a jackboot—which might explain their marriage. Opposites attract, and all that.

"Hi, Mike! Good to meet you! What brings you to Paradise?"

I explained my mission, extending water infrastructure. How I'd wanted to take some time out after ten years as a Civil Engineering contractor in the States. I didn't tell them my fiancée left me for my best friend. Nor that I'd lost my last contracting gig after I showed up for work drunk when she walked out. Punched a hole in my locker and smashed the pool cues to pieces in the mess room before they dragged me to the office and fired me.

* * * *

The police arrived from Tahiti right after Janine's body was found—and the press came with them. There are no hotels on Hiva-Oa, just guest houses or government-run hostels. The one bar in Atuona doubles as a restaurant and general store. It's filled with an odd mixture of traditional French produce, local staples like coconut butter and rice and the worst kind of American junk food.

After the murder, the stores and bar and guest houses were stuffed with officials and drunks. Atuona being so small, everyone knew when Janine's husband was whisked from the church up on the hill and down to the police station, then arrested and tossed into a cell. The fishermen took a long time tidying their nets that day. And the expats suddenly had to buy lots of groceries and do lots of drinking. I'll admit I was curious too. So, I rolled down to the bar a little earlier than usual to find out what rumors were running.

As I approached the bar, a blue building with holes where doors and windows should be, I saw the paper-thin form of Alexandre perched at the bar. Alexandre was a fixture on the cocktail party circuit. His loudly professed devotion to God sat ill with his habit of muttering unvarnished insights about other expats' behavior when drunk, a *Gitanes* pinched between his first two fingers, cigarette held aloft at an obtuse angle.

"*Mon vieux*," he sing-songed as I entered the bar. I sat down on the stool next to his. He lowered his voice. "I heard he beat her to death. They say he caught her playing *bagatelle* with another man."

Alexandre gave me a knowing look like I would understand the French word. Then he sucked greedily on his cigarette and stubbed it out on the bar. He turned to the barman and said something about "*la même chose.*" I also heard, "*une bière pour Michel.*"

Behind the bar, Désiré smiled to himself and fixed Alexandre another cocktail. He didn't know much more French than me, being more interested in drill rap and hip-hop. Any time I'd been in there by myself, he bugged me about how to get a visa for the US.

Désiré yanked open the fridge and popped a 333 Export Beer, known as a "*trent-trois,*" down on the flaking wooden bar in front of me, rolling his eyes at the old fellow's campy gossip. Alexandre watched my reaction, his next cigarette already smoldering between his fingers.

"What you think? It is the husband, *non*? Who else? One of these locals?" He tut-tutted. "Ah no, my friend. They are too timid, too agreeable. Incapable of crime. It must have been one of we few civilized."

I took a pull at my beer and looked round the bar at the assorted journalists and policemen, locals, and ex-pats. I recognized most of the locals and knew all the ex-pats by name. Any one of these men—and they were mostly men—could have done it.

Janine was the only person on the island who would sashay into the supermarket looking like she'd just stepped off the catwalk. Most of us went in wearing shorts and a T-shirt, hunting that elusive rarity—milk fresh from Hiva-Oa's tiny dairy. And then there were those looks she gave me. Maybe she gave them to other men too.

* * * *

The second cocktail party invitation came two weeks after the first. When I received it, I didn't realize these invitations were designed to stave off boredom for the ex-pat community—or that I'd end up receiving dozens of them. After the Governor's cocktail party, I'd been established as *"fréquentable,"* and now, whether I wanted it or not, I was part of the crowd.

This party was at Madame Abeille's wooden home, nestled among thick foliage in the hills above the harbor. Her deck creaked worryingly when the party was in full swing but offered a panorama of Atuona's main drag: the supermarket/bar/restaurant. The police station. To your far left, looking down, the faded grandeur of the Governor's residence on an isthmus jutting into the harbor. And away to the right, overlooking it all, the Catholic church on the lower slopes of Temetiu, its huge cross featuring Christ in his agony.

The others were already there by the time I arrived at the party clutching a bottle of wino-cheap Australian chardonnay. Madame Abeille expressed such delight at my meagre gift, as if I'd brought a bottle of Chateau de Something Expensive. An air-kiss on each cheek, then she ushered me through her house and out to the deck.

Ian McLennan sat on a low cane sofa, debating the finer points of some French theologian's work with Alexandre. He spoke with loud authority while Alexandre nodded and smoked. The governor stood some way off, holding court with a bevy of locals. I accepted a Mint Julep from Madame Abeille—"This night, we are proposing an American cocktail in your honor"—her kohl'd eyes wrinkling. I knocked back half my drink and went to take in the view from the railing.

I finished my Julep and Janine was behind me. I smelled cigarette smoke and turned around: my heart jolted when I saw her high heels, light check skirt, and tight maroon top.

"Michael! I could have told you we'd meet again soon," she laughed. "After all, Atuona is the center of the known universe!" She glanced at her husband, still deep in conversation with the desiccated Alexandre. Then she leaned in. "Come keep me company. I'm going to be naughty, and I need someone to talk to."

She led me back through the house, out the front door and around the side where the garden pitched down towards the village. A patch of grass ended in some blooming rhododendrons that gave way to thick jungle.

"Careful! Step too far that way and we'll never see you again. Now, I'm going to smoke and you're going to tell me all about you."

She leaned back against the side of Madame Abeille's house and pulled a pack of cigarettes and a lighter out of her clutch bag. She lit up, drew deeply on her cigarette.

"So: why Atuona? Why come all this way?"

Before I could answer, she snickered to herself. "The impulse to do good in the world just overcame you, right?" A pause. "Believe me, I know all about that from Ian."

Another pull on her cigarette, a little laugh. She looked off over the trees where the sun was setting. I started giving her the usual lines about my career. By the end of her cigarette, I'd told her about my relationship with Maureen, my ex. How I needed to escape, and how two years with the Peace Corps sounded ideal. And she'd told me about herself—mid-Western girl who married a mid-Western boy, "and became a baby-making machine. And after that, he wanted control. And that's what he still wants."

She exhaled a cloud of smoke, and I thought I saw a tear forming in her eye.

"So, I guess we two exiles should stick together, huh?"

Then she put her arms around my neck and hugged me. I didn't respond at first. I may not have moved, but I wanted her, and she knew it.

"You'll probably like it here," she said, arms still around my neck. "But then, you're not married to a religious maniac. *The husband is the head of the wife, and she shall submit to him.*"

She leaned back, keeping her arms on my shoulders. Her hips came closer to mine, and I felt her heat.

"Ephesians Chapter Five, in case you're wondering. It's one of my husband's favorites. Just don't ask me which verse. Ian would probably punch a hole in the wall if I got it wrong—he usually does."

She moved her head closer to mine. Then noise from the front of the house. A woman stood watching us—as I later found out, it was Madame Abeille's maid, Alice. Janine removed her arms from around my neck and began speaking rapid French to Alice. I heard the word *"rien"* several times. Alice turned her slender form toward the house and went inside without a word. Janine's hand brushed against mine.

"I think it's time for us to go back, Michael. Let's stay in touch."

* * * *

Over time, I became dulled to these islands' beauty—as Janine predicted. Yes, they sound like paradise to anyone stuck in the middle of a big city: simple, beautiful jewels where nothing ever happens, rising out of turquoise waters that flash with sunlight.

The fact that nothing ever happened here explained the endless cocktail parties, the gossip, and the bitchery. That, and the absence of fraternization between ex-pats and locals. As the months wore on and my boredom worsened, I did my best to change that situation. It was easier for me to integrate because I was working with local laborers on the new water system. Plus, the young guys all wanted to move to the States. A couple of times a week I'd find myself in the bar, struggling to make myself understood in a mixture of patois, French, and English. I tried to tell them they were better off staying, but they wouldn't listen.

Apart from making friends with the locals, boredom led me to fantasize about Janine. We'd barely spoken since that second cocktail party, but something drew me in. Something more than her looks, her touch. And it didn't go unnoticed by those around us, either.

* * * *

One week, the cocktail circuit landed at the home of Michelle and Eric, two professionals who'd escaped metropolitan France to be the elementary teacher and district health professional on Hiva-Oa. If other expats were trying to live out some colonial fantasy sixty years too late, Michelle and Eric were the opposite—they'd learned *Reo Mā'ohi* and spoke it loudly to the locals. Still, they weren't above taking part in the expat cocktail circuit—or employing a maid and cook to serve them.

Twenty minutes after their party started at five-thirty, the drink was raging. Having observed the decorum of waiting until five p.m., it looked like everyone was going to soak themselves sick before leaving around seven.

My hostess, Michelle, dragged me out to look at their bougainvillea, imported from South America and meticulously cultivated. After passing a few pleasantries, she grabbed my forearm.

"Michael," she whispered. "Be careful! People talk of you and the young American!"

"What? I barely ever speak to her. What are they saying?"

"Oh, come, Michael. Not with me. Everyone knows you were seen embracing her by the maid of Madame Abeille. In France we say that if this is in public, *alors…*"

Her words tailed off and she let go of my arm. "This Ian, her husband—you know how jealous Americans can be. And he is very…influential with the governor, I tell you."

I hesitated, then thanked her and we went back inside.

* * * *

Out on the veranda, Ian led the ex-pats in grace—preparing them with God's blessing for their next meal. His midwestern vowels mangled the French words, even to my untrained ear: "*Beynis-ez nouz, Seygnieur, et bey-*

nis-ez le repast que nouz all ons prender. Oh name du Pair, du Fills, et du Saing Esprit. Amen."

Ian looked up as I entered, then turned his face away to the sea, deep as a well in the bay window. Janine shot me a look, hands cupped and head bowed. My heart twisted again.

That was the last cocktail party I attended for a while.

* * * *

I next saw Janine at the start of Easter week—Palm Sunday. Palm fronds being abundant, the Catholic church held a parade with townsfolk holding up palms by the side of the route. The parade led from the *Mairie* along the sea-front and up the hill to the church. Although there was still a week of Lent left, the fishermen in the harbor, and many others, used the parade as an excuse to hit the "*trente-trois*" and palm wine.

A committed atheist, I hung out with the fishermen to watch the parade, drinking near their boats, the nets reeking of brine and kelp. Ian McLennan paraded just after the *curé* and his assistants in a show of Christian unity, Janine demure by his side and their three little kids behind, immaculate in white shirts and dark shorts. She wore a sun hat, round Jackie O shades, and an expensive white dress cut just below the knee.

An older fisherman muttered something I didn't understand that sounded like "*baize*," cigarette in one hand and a clear cup of palm wine in the other.

"What's that?"

After nearly a year here, my French hadn't improved much. One of the younger fishermen stuck himself between me and the old guy.

"Him say she fine, feel me?" He spoke with a Polynesian accent, cheap gold earrings dangling from his lobes, homestyle tattoos of Tupac and Biggie Smalls on his arms.

The old guy yammered some mix of patois, French and *Reo Mā'ohi*. I looked at the young guy.

"He say her trouble soon come. Half the men in the village is sprung for her. Says her husband need watch his back, haha!"

Then this wannabe gangsta rapper took his gutting knife and drove it hard into the prow of his boat.

"Sometimes the woman need correction in her thinking. Her husband should realize it."

Then he spat on the sand and glared at me, his brown pupils fierce. I shrugged my shoulders, hiding my thoughts.

* * * *

After the Easter week service, which I didn't attend (a major mark against me, as I later discovered) the expats gathered at the Governor's house for drinks. The idea of another cocktail party with the same crew sounded as boring as the day is long, but I still showed. That's the thing about small-town places: you do almost everything out of habit, or to avoid pissing others off—or both.

Seated in a rattan chair on the governor's veranda, I swallowed a rocket-fuel gin and tonic in record time, wondering how soon I could ask for another. Then I saw Janine in her white dress and sun hat. Ian stood in a group with Madame Abeille, Eric, Michelle, and some others, no doubt chatting local politics.

Janine approached and I stood up, my lips brushing her cheek in greeting. I caught a hint of her honeysuckle perfume, her foundation, that scent of tobacco and alcohol.

"Michael," she said. Those eyes. "So good to see you again. What a day!"

She told me their nanny had Sundays off, so the children had been forced to attend the Easter Parade. Now they were sleeping off a treat lunch of pizza and ice cream at home, watched by the *curé*'s housekeeper.

"…and Ian's been pontificating at me as usual about smoking and the demon alcohol. But all that church gave me space to think about something."

"What about?" I asked, motioning at one of the Governor's staff to serve Janine another white wine.

"Thank you," she said to the liveried server, then waited until he was out of earshot. She bent her head slightly toward me, her back to her husband. "I'm thinking about how I'd like to get you alone, take your clothes off and screw you 'til you go blind."

Still with her back to the others, she told me where she wanted to meet that night, down on the beach at two a.m. I went and met her there, and we did what we wanted to do. Things carried on like that for a while—until her husband found out.

* * * *

The phone in my bungalow never rang. I always used my cell phone for work or when I'm calling the States. So, I knew something was wrong when it started ringing late one evening.

"Michael," a voice hissed. It was Janine.

"What is it?"

"This has to end. This…thing between us. He knows. He's going to kill me."

"What?"

"I'm heading for the beach. Come meet me."

I checked my watch. It was ten-thirty. I could be there in twenty minutes. We arranged to meet below the Governor's residence where the sand met the rocks at the bottom of some cliffs. But I never showed up. And I never found out if she showed up, either.

When I reached the harbor front, I realized we'd arranged to meet way too early in the evening. The bar hadn't closed, and my fishermen buddies still hung around, mostly drunk. It was Friday, which meant no one was working tomorrow, and the locals were taking full advantage. My usual thing was to have a couple of beers after work and then go home to eat, and I'd stupidly thought everyone else did the same—but no. Fridays were party time in downtown Atuona.

To avoid suspicion and because I was a little early, I took a cup of palm and a beer with my buddies. The old guy who'd foretold trouble for Janine was there, as was Mr. Wannabe Gangsta. They had a driftwood brazier going, and some old French pop music station out of Tahiti on the radio. No sooner had I drunk my cup of palm than the police arrived and told us to go home or head back to the bar across the street.

I took my friends across the road for a drink—okay, three drinks—and by the time I got to where I was supposed to meet Janine, she was gone. I'd texted her to say I was going to be late, but never got a reply. So, I went back to the bar and had a few more.

When I got kicked out after midnight, I think I tried to go looking for her. I say "I think" because I blacked out and woke up the next day on a bench at the seafront. I was covered in dust and mud, my pants ripped at the knees. I had dirt under my nails and my hands were cut and scratched. I must have fallen over or something.

Then, on my way back to my bungalow, I received a text message from Alexandre that said Janine was dead.

* * * *

The knock on my door came four days after the police arrived. They'd found out about my affair with Janine. Not just from the gossiping expats, but also from an examination of my mobile phone records. They'd read the text messages between us. I tried to tell them about the call to my apartment on the landline, but they just smiled and nodded like they'd heard it all before.

They took me from the interview room across the corridor to the cells. They opened the door of a cell and shoved me inside. I looked out the window to see old Alexandre joking and laughing with that young fisherman with the hip-hop tattoos and the violent knife. It was then I realized that I'd been set up—and I wasn't the only one who was going to suffer.

✗

J.W. Wood's (https://jwwoodwriter.net) poems, stories and articles have appeared widely in the US, UK, Canada, and beyond. The author of six books of poems and a thriller, his first book of short stories will appear from AN Editions in the UK in September 2024. His work has received awards in the US, Canada, and India.

MOST IMPORTANT MEAL OF THE DAY

R.T. LAWTON

So, I'm sitting in the Boca del Toro, a nice family-owned Mexican restaurant down off lower Broadway, a few blocks west of where the subway comes out. The word nice having to do with the restaurant, not the family what owns it. And, I'm here way early in the morning not only because the food is good, but Sarah the cashier has eyes for me, in which case, she always gives me for free, a breakfast burrito she makes up from the previous night's leftovers. A little *carne* from here, some *frijoles* from there, a dab of *queso*, some salsa and a spare tortilla that her boss won't miss from inventory. There's also a scrambled egg or two stuffed into the tortilla with everything else, but I doubt the owner, even as tight as he is with money, bothers to count individual eggs in the carton. As long as we are careful, there should be no problems.

For all this, because times are tough and I am recently unemployed and winter is not far off, I make eyes back at her and maybe pay my way by leaving her a little love poem in Spanish. She don't speak or understand the Spanish, but thinks my poems are great, especially if I read them to her in my native tongue. Something about my accent seems to get her all tingly.

Anyways, I'm trying to hurry up and get out before the owner shows up, cuz he will know just by looking at me that I am not a paying customer, which will get Sarah in trouble and there will go my breakfasts for free. And, we all know that breakfast is the most important meal of the day. Especially if it's the only meal of the day you're getting. No way do I want to mess this up.

I am almost finished with my last cup of Colombian coffee brewed strong the way I like it and with a little cream poured in it to lighten up the color, when I look over the rim of my cup and see two guys peeking in the big front window. One of them waves at me and the other opens the front door that Sarah forgot to lock behind me after I came in. Here them two come, headed right for my table.

Needless to say, I am not too happy to see this Leonard and this Jules. Everyone in this part of the city knows they are nothing more than burglars. It will not enhance my reputation to be seen in their company, plus the restaurant owner will be coming to work any time now.

I stand up to leave.

Jules puts his hand on my shoulder, reseats me and then sits himself in the chair beside me.

Leonard pulls out the chair on the other side of the table and sits himself down over there. They look friendly in the face, but who knows these days. Times are tough all over.

I don't wish to appear unfriendly, but I also don't want them to get the idea that we are boon companions of some sort, so I try for the middle ground and fall back on the common street greeting.

"What's up?"

"It's like this, Mexican Bob," says Leonard, "we've got a proposition for you."

Now, I don't know propositions from prepositions in English, but whatever they got in mind can't be good for my future. Besides which, I got to get them and me out of here, quick like a bunny, as these *norte-americanos* say.

Tick. Tock. The clock is literally ticking where I can see it on the wall.

I am desperate, so I make a choice. Okay, it may not be the best choice, but I am under a lot of pressure just now cuz Immigration has been looking at me sideways for any reason they can find to put me on one of their green buses with stiff-wire window screens for a one-way ride south.

This Leonard and Jules are trouble I don't need right at this time. It would be better for me to be seen as a dissociate of theirs instead of an associate if I wish to stay in this city of new possibilities.

"Gentlemen," I say to them, "could we take this discussion to my office out in the alley?"

Jules looks around us.

"It's late October and a bit cold out there. What's wrong with in here?"

"There's a certain someone who will show up shortly and he will not be happy to see me on his premises. As he is a guy with violent tendencies toward those peoples he does not like, it would be best to remove ourselves from his sight before he even sees us."

Leonard and Jules look at each other.

Jules nods his head.

Leonard now has his own forehead scrunched up in a frown like he is having trouble in his contemplating as he says to me, "I didn't know you kept an office out in the alley. How long you been doing that?"

I do not wish to insult his intelligence ability, so I merely reply, "Since I lost my job two weeks ago as dishwasher at fancy restaurant in mid-town. And, because of that, it seems the rent out back of here is a very affordable price for an office if one can ignore the ambience."

Leonard opens his mouth to say something, but Jules and I stand up and head for the back door before he can get started with whatever. Looking back over my shoulder, I see Sarah at the table checking my wadded-up paper napkin and then under my empty plate to see if I leave her another love poem this morning. Actually, I had one in mind from a poetry book I was reading in the city library yesterday, but with these two burglars interrupting my breakfast, I didn't have time to write it out on a napkin in person like I usually do for her. Now, I will owe her two love poems if I wish to continue eating at this dining establishment. And, it will probably be poem payment up front for that next breakfast, if I can still get it.

Out in the alley, I smell the old grease from the restaurant grill, the rancid garbage in the dumpsters and a strong whiff of stale smoke off the cook's growing pile of discarded cigarette butts just outside the back door from when he takes a break from cooking.

The rear door slams shut and now it's just the three of us out here in the cold.

I decide I may as well get this over with, so as I can get on with the rest of my day.

"What is this preposition you have for me?"

Leonard gives me a funny look and then turns to Jules for guidance.

"It's not a preposition," replies Jules, "it's a potential business venture up for discussion."

"You are offering me a job," I say. "Thas nice, but I don't do burglary things. I have no wish to engender my standing as an honest citizen in this beautiful country."

Jules puts his hands, palm out, about chest high and waves them slightly from side to side.

"No, no," he reassures me, "we don't want you to steal anything. We just want you to give us some information."

Now, the thought occurs to me that if I make enough money selling them this information, whatever it is, then maybe I can buy Sarah a little sack of high-class chocolates to go with the next love poems. Then, in her heart, she will find it easier to forgive me for not having left her some sweet words on paper at the table this morning.

"How much will this business venture you have in mind pay me?"

"That depends," says Leonard.

"On what?" I ask.

"First," says Jules, "you have to give us good information so we can do a particular job. Then, we see how much cash we end up with on that job. And then, you get a percentage of the action."

"Oh," I say, "a *mordida*, a little bite of the pie. It is something like back home when rich land developer gives money to a politician to get the proper zoning he needs. Now I see."

"What are you talking about?" asks Leonard. "We're not buying real estate here."

Jules puts a hand on Leonard's arm.

"Relax," he says. Then he turns back to me.

"You don't have to do nothing, except provide us some information. Period. And then, you get a piece of whatever we get. Okay?"

"How big a piece of whatever?"

"A tenth."

In my mind, I'm thinking like these guys are going to hit a place for a thousand dollars and I will get a hundred dollars for myself out of the deal. Easy money. I can then buy Sarah an even bigger sack of chocolates than I thought.

"Okay, so what information do I give you?"

"Where does he keep the money?"

I don't know who they are talking about, so I figure we need to get this straight before we continue.

"Who is this *he* you are asking about?"

"The man who owns this restaurant."

"Oh, so you are talking about the money he makes each day from serving the Mexican food to peoples who eat in his establishment."

I do not like this idea.

"No can do," I say.

"Why not?" asks Leonard.

"Because, if Mister Gordo loses all his restaurant money and goes broke, then Sarah will lose her job and I will lose my breakfasts for free."

"No, no, no," says Jules in a soothing tone. "We won't touch the restaurant money he keeps in that small safe by his office desk. We're talking about the other money."

"Oh, okay then."

I think about this for a minute.

"What other money are we talking about here?"

"Don't worry about it," says Jules. He pats me on the shoulder like we are old friends. "What we want to know, is does he have a second safe, a very large one? Like maybe a walk-in safe?"

I shake my head.

"I never see no second safe."

Jules reaches into his pocket and takes out five ten-dollar bills. I know there are five of them because he fans them out where I can see them better.

"Too bad," he says. "We were thinking about paying you some cash in advance of you getting your ten percent of whatever we get."

Then a memory of something I once see pops into my head. Maybe it's got a relation to what these two are interested in. It wouldn't hurt to mention this thing and see.

"Wait, wait," I say. "There is one morning, the owner come in early with two rough men and then Sarah has to quick hide me in another room. All three men were carrying gym bags that appeared to be very heavy, but these men don't look like the type who go to gyms."

Jules arched his left eyebrow and moved a little closer to me.

"Go on."

"They carry the bags through the dining room and into the office. When their voices sound far away, you know, muffled, Sarah decides it is time to sneak me out of the restaurant."

"What do you mean their voices sounded muffled?"

"I am a little curious, so as Sarah is hustling me out, I look back over my shoulder. These men are standing in a very small room behind the office. The funny thing is that this large bookcase on the back wall of the office is swung open to one side like a big door."

"A hidden room," says Leonard. "I knew it."

"Was there a steel door to this room behind the bookcase?" asks Jules.

"It is smooth like a metal door, but I don't see any combination dials like a vault has. Just a single handle and a hole for a large key."

Jules holds up one index finger as if to say, "Give me a minute." Then he and Leonard go to the other side of the alley, huddle together and whisper for a short time.

When they come back to where I'm standing, Jules hands me one of the ten-dollar bills. The rest of them he holds close to his chest, just out of my reach.

"That's a start," he says. "What else you got?"

I don't know what else they are looking for, but that ten dollars is nice to have in my hand, so I think a while.

"This happen on a Friday morning," I finally say and then look carefully at them to see if I am going the right direction.

Jules nods his head slightly and hands me another ten-dollar bill.

"I remember now," I say, "it is always on a Friday morning that I see the owner coming to work with a gym bag in his hand. Usually, I am through eating and already out the door when I see owner walk by me on the sidewalk."

Jules hands me a third ten.

I am starting to feel like contestant on television quiz show and having right answers to questions.

"What about the other two guys?" asks Leonard. "You see them again?"

"Only twice other times. Both times also on Friday mornings. Same peoples carrying gym bags, it is always gym bags."

I stick my hand out.

Jules gives me a fourth ten.

I am start to smile now, cuz I haven't had this much dollars at one time since I am unemployed dishwasher at fancy restaurant. Maybe I am going to have lucky day today.

"One more question for now," says Jules. "Is the owner going to close up his restaurant for the Day of the Dead?"

This is easy question, so mine is easy answer.

"Sure, sure," I say. "*Dia de los Muertos* is traditional Mexican holiday to honor deceased members of the family. He will take food and drink to the cemetery. The whole family will go."

"How do you know this about the family?"

"Sarah tells me I get no breakfast that day. Restaurant closed, everybody go to cemetery. She not family, but owner say she go with them to take care of the food they eat that day. This all-day deal."

"And the cook?"

"Cook go too. Mister Gordo take small charcoal grill for cook in cemetery."

I put my hand out for last ten-dollar bill.

Leonard reaches over to Jules, plucks the tenner out of his hand, and tears the ten-dollar bill in half. He then gives me one of the torn halves.

"What is this?" I ask.

"We want you to stick around," says Leonard, "in case we need to ask more questions later. We don't want you to take a runner on us."

My smile is now gone. I frown at him.

"I am already in land of opportunity. I don't run anywhere."

Leonard stuffed the other half of the torn tenner in his shirt pocket.

"You'll get this when we pay you the rest of the money. In the meantime, don't say nothing to nobody else about this."

I have four ten-dollar bills in my left hand, along with half of the ten that is torn into two pieces. And, I have my right hand back out sticking into empty air, when Leonard and Jules turn and walk away.

"It's a week until Dead Day," Leonard throws back over his shoulder. "We'll be in touch."

And, then they are down the alley and gone.

* * * *

Me, I don't hear nothing from these two burglars for the next several days. I start thinking maybe they change their mind about doing this job and that's a good thing. Not that I don't want my ten percent of whatever, but the more I ruminate on the questions those two ask me, the more I think is trouble for Sarah and me and those tasty breakfasts. For now, I am already back in Sarah's good graces. I buy those fancy chocolates for Sarah and copy down two love poems from a library book and give them to her that very next day after the meeting in my office in alley. She and I are back on track again for breakfast. In the days since Leonard and Jules first come to see me, life is almost returning to normal. Trouble is problem I don't need.

We are now one day after the Day of the Dead and I go to restaurant early this morning, but sign in window say restaurant is closed even though this is second day of being closed, if I count the holiday itself. I put hand up to forehead, shield eyes and look through window, but no Sarah, nobody moving around inside. I wait across street for couple hours. Nobody go in or out, so I walk to library, find something to do, keep mind busy. I will return to restaurant early in morning tomorrow. See if open yet.

But, for now is library. It is place I go to read newspapers to practice my English. While I am sitting at a table reading, Gracious John in his full-length tan trench coat approaches from the opposite side. This John is a homeless man who gets his nickname from his polite manners. Nobody seems to know if this extreme politeness comes from him being raised by gracious parents or if he is once a doorman for the Waldorf or some other such high-class establishment.

John politely inquires in a soft voice if he may sit down across the table from me.

I gesture at him to sit, so he pulls out a chair, dusts it off with his white handkerchief, refolds the handkerchief and sits. John is one of those people who keeps his ear to the street and generally knows almost everything going on in this town, sometimes even before the event, whatever it is, happens to happen.

"Did you hear what takes place at the Boca del Toro Restaurant?" he asks in his soft voice.

Right away, I am worry about Sarah because the restaurant is still closed this morning when I go there. My voice therefore probably rises a little louder than it should in this quiet place.

"Tell me," I say.

"Shhhh," whispers the elderly lady behind the reference desk. "People in the library need their silence to study."

Cautiously, I look around me. There is nobody here, except us three. I smile and nod at her.

Gracious John softens his voice even more than before. I have to lean partway across the table to hear him.

"Yesterday, the restaurant was burgled. It was a semi-professional job as these things go. They disabled the alarms as they should and came in through the back door. Then, they went to the office, swung a large bookcase open and used a torch on the metal door in order to get into a small room behind the office."

My mind immediately focuses on Leonard and Jules. They do this thing after all. I now need to be careful.

"This is news to me," I say. "Do the police know who does this?"

"The police were not notified," says John, "but other parties are putting pieces together."

Real quick, I am wondering who does not call police when their business is burgled?

"What other parties are we talking about here?"

"I do not like to put the touch on you," John apologizes, "but I have not eaten in two days, and there are those who know you get breakfasts for free."

I always agree with people when they say how gracious Gracious John can be, but I never know how subtle he can also be when putting the touch on someone.

"What else do *they* know, John?"

"Well," he says, "they know you come into some money recently."

Okay, so somebody sees me out in the alley speaking with this Leonard and this Jules, two known burglars, and the word has spread.

"Who is other parties, John?"

Gracious John hangs his head slightly and looks at me with his big brown, sad eyes. He looks like big dog silently begging for scraps from table.

I reach in pants pocket and carefully finger out one of the tens I have folded over double like someone would if he had a money clip to hold his money in. All I have is a large oblong wire clip used to hold papers together. I wrestle the ten-dollar bill out of the oversized paper clip so as John cannot see how much dollars is left, and I slid the bill carefully across the tabletop.

The bill disappears like John has a vacuum hose up his sleeve. That's when I decide to never play poker games with Gracious John, just in case he has some bad habits with cards I don't know about. Other than that, people say Gracious John is a very honest guy.

John looks around like he is checking to see if anyone is eavesdropping.

"The parties of which we speak," says John, "are those connected to the Gulf Coast Mexico Cartel. They are said to bring many illegal substances to this city."

These are people I have no wish to get acquainted with in this country and even much less so in my old country.

"What do they have to do with Mister Gordo?"

"Mister Gordo launders the money they make from those illegal substances."

"Oh."

Then I think, if they know of my meeting with this Leonard and this Jules, then they would want me in the cemetery pretty darn quick. Truth be known, I do not wish to have my own personal Day of the Dead.

"Do they know who burgled the restaurant?"

John shakes his head.

"Not yet."

"Do you know how much money the burglars got?"

"Hard to tell," says John, "their torch got too hot on the metal door and much of the money in the hidden room caught fire. It took them a while to find a fire extinguisher and put it out."

I lean back in my chair. This is definitely not lucky day for me.

"Thanks, John."

He gives me that sad, dog-eyed look again as if he thinks he deserves a bigger touch for the information he just gives me.

I reach in my pocket again and feel the torn half of the ten-dollar bill. Carefully, I extract it, fold it over twice under the table and then bring it out to let John see the corner with the numeral ten in it.

"One more thing, John," I say. "Do you know where this Leonard and this Jules are these days?"

"Leonard tells a friend of his that he and Jules are going to San Francisco to visit Leonard's sick mother, but Jules tells a close relative that he and Leonard are flying to Las Vegas to work in a casino. Personally, I do not know of Leonard having a mother, sick or otherwise, in California and neither Leonard nor Jules are good enough at handling cards or dice to work in any gambling establishment. So, the answer to your question is no."

Then, John sticks his hand out like he is expecting something anyway.

It is a feeling I know well, so I shrug and hand him the torn half on the tenner.

He unfolds the bill, looks at it, then looks at me and then back at the bill again.

"You get the other half," I say, "when I get some money which is owed to me by certain parties we both know."

Gracious John scoots back his chair, stands and walks away shaking his head sadly and staring at that half of a ten-dollar bill not even worth five dollars in the condition it now is.

* * * *

Two more weeks have passed, and I have relocated to a different library just in case this Mister Gordo and his Gulf Coast peoples are looking for me. I always say that given enough time I can explain anything, but actually, it is better to not be found in first place and then have to explain anything.

So, once again I am sitting at table reading newspapers, when I get a tap on shoulder, and I almost turn over the chair I am sitting in.

"We have business to conduct," says a soft voice I recognize as belonging to Gracious John.

As my nerves settle back down, I motion for him to join me.

John walks around the table and pulls out a chair on other side.

I suspect he wants to watch my facial reactions while we talk. Everyone always say Gracious John is good at reading tells.

He dusts off the chair seat with his white handkerchief, refolds it and puts it away before sitting.

I lean forward and whisper.

"What's up, Gracious John?"

"I run into some friends of yours a day ago," he says in a low voice, "and they wish me to give you something before they take a long vacation in parts unknown."

He reaches into an inside pocket of his trench coat, and I would flinch, but I don't know John, up to now, to be a violent type of guy. Still, I am thinking where exits are, just in case.

John brings out something from his pocket, covers it with his hand and slides this something over the tabletop to me.

I cover it with my hand, bend it upward and look at it. It is eight one-hundred-dollar bills. They appear to be blackened on one end as if once scorched.

"What is this?" I ask him.

"Jules tells me you would know. Something about your little bite of the pie."

"Oh," I say. "Did he say anything else?"

"Yes," says John and he brought something else out his inside pocket and slides it across the tabletop. "He says this is also yours now,"

I look and it is the other half of the torn ten-dollar bill.

John looks at me with his big, sad-dog eyes again.

"I have not eaten for two days," he says.

I think about it for a while. John is honest to give me all this money, so I separate one of the scorched one-hundred-dollar bills and slide it across the table to him.

He looks at it and slides it back.

"Do you have anything smaller?"

Not anymore. I have long ago spent the other ten-dollar bills that Jules gave me as an advance on whatever. Then I remember the half of the torn ten-dollar bill I give Gracious John a few weeks ago and now I have the other half in my hand. I slide it across the table.

He looks at this second torn half and smiles his thanks. Now Gracious John has both halves and can cash it in for full face value. He stands up to leave, then pauses, puts both hands on the tabletop and leans forward.

"By the way," he says, "I see Sarah a couple of days ago. She has a new job and tells me you should come in early some morning for breakfast."

He gives me a business card with a name and address printed on the card.

"It's the Sitting Duck Restaurant over in China Town," he says, "and I hear it's owned by some triad."

Then he is gone.

I am thinking I will be glad to see Sarah again and get back to my breakfasts for free. Tomorrow will be a good day to go and maybe take some poems and a couple of flowers. I do not know what Chinese peoples eat for breakfast, but food is food. My stomach will be happy again. What do I care if this Chinese restaurant is owned by one persons or by three? Three triad peoples as owners can't be any worse than Mister Gordo and Gulf Coast Cartel.

Breakfasts for free again is most important thing.

R.T. Lawton is a retired federal law enforcement agent, past member of the Mystery Writers of America board of directors, a 2022 Edgar Award winner for Best Short Story, and has over 160 short stories in various anthologies and other publications, to include 51 sold to *Alfred Hitchcock's Mystery Magazine*. He currently has nine short story collections in paperback and e-format for purchase on Amazon.

LUXURY GOODS

R.M. LOWERY

She nearly whispered the order to the bartender. Virgin mojito, extra mint. Bars are unpopular places to not drink alcohol.

It was a nice place. Modern and trendy with funky carpets, pops of color everywhere, and lots of mid-century modern touches. Smooth jazz played softly from speakers tucked into the high ceilings as the bartender placed a napkin on the bar in front of her. Moments later, he set her drink on the napkin.

Settling into one of the padded stools, she sipped the drink, allowing the minty taste to transport her to an exotic location, someplace more interesting than a hotel bar near the airport.

Reaching for her cell phone, she offered a quick smile to the man at the end of the bar. He'd been staring at her since she walked in. Now he'd moved on from staring to checking her up and down. Nothing about her outfit was provocative, just a dark blue flare dress with a split collar. For a plain button-up dress, it always seemed to gain lots of attention from guys, probably because it had a school-girl look to it, which seemed to ignite a particular fantasy in their minds.

From her periphery, she noticed his eyes had shifted to her knee-high suede boots. For a moment, at least. His eyes soon began scanning up her legs, then to her ass, then to her breasts.

She could move, sure. Maybe grab a table somewhere out of his gaze, but he seemed harmless. Probably just a lonely, horny business traveler.

She looked at him. He seemed embarrassed that she'd caught him staring at her chest. She offered another slight smile before returning her attention to her phone.

He was attractive, even if his hairline was beginning to betray him. He wasn't handsome or stunning, necessarily, but he seemed to be in good shape. He was, however, probably close to double her age. She guessed late forties, maybe early fifties. So maybe not *double* her age, but even if he was only forty-five, that still meant eighteen years separated them, which was probably exciting for him.

Laughing to herself about men and their weird thoughts, she returned to her phone and began mindlessly scrolling through Instagram, dream-shopping for a new wardrobe for this summer, which was still a good three months away.

It seemed he'd taken her last smile as some kind of invitation and was now standing to her right, a couple stool-lengths away. She pretended not to notice.

Eventually he said, "You just passing through too, I take it?"

It was an awkward pick-up line, but probably not for a guy his age. She turned her head to him and said, "I'm sorry?"

"Oh, I was just wondering if you're staying here on business, or if you're from the area."

She offered him another smile, a reward for putting a pathetic spin on the classic *"are you from around here?"*

He seemed like a nice guy, so she went along with his attempt at conversation and said, "I'm waiting for a flight."

He smiled an awkward smile, his teeth straight and bright, likely the result of regular whitening treatments. She smiled back and threw him an easy one, saying, "How about you? Business travel?"

"Yeah. Third time this month I've been here."

The TravisMathew shirt he wore said that he probably liked golf, and the well-fitted dress slacks it was paired with along with the Ted Baker belt indicated a woman probably selected his outfits for him.

He leaned against the bar and said, "So, you traveling for business as well?"

"No. I'm trying to get back to New England after visiting my grandmother in Florida. I was supposed to grab a connecting flight here, so I ran across the airport—in heeled boots nonetheless—to have someone at the gate tell me that my flight had been canceled. So, I'm stranded here until tomorrow."

"Oh, wow. That sucks. I've had that happen." He laughed a fake laugh. "I mean, not the running in heels part."

She pretended to laugh.

He motioned to an empty stool. "You mind?"

She shook her head, and he pulled out the stool. Once settled, he extended his hand and said, "I'm Steven."

She shook his hand. "Jess."

"Nice to meet you, Jess. Sorry your trip isn't going well."

"I've only told you the first part." She chuckled darkly. "Most of my luggage is on its way to a city I'm not in. Then, I'd thought I'd gotten a reservation at a hotel, so I took an Uber there only to learn they somehow didn't have me in their system, and the place was booked solid. So, then I Ubered over here, and luckily, I got a room, but when I got to the room, I realized I didn't have my debit card. The last place I remember having it was the first Uber, but I haven't been able to get hold of that driver, so I ended up just canceling the card."

He exhaled a long breath slowly. "Okay. That takes the cake. For as much as I've traveled, I don't think I've ever had a day that bad. You were able to get a room though? Even without your card?"

"Yeah. It was just my debit card, and thankfully my credit card was still in my bag." She motioned to the brown leather Coach bag on the stool next to her. "But needless to say, it's been a long day."

"I'm very sorry."

He asked where she was from, and she told him Portland, Maine. He'd never been, but he'd like to visit because he'd heard it was beautiful. She told him it was. Steven was from Northern California, a town named Lodi in between Sacramento and Stockton. He liked it, he said.

Finishing a sip of his drink, he said, "The weather's about perfect. Wish it was closer to a good beach though."

She nodded and sipped her drink. The gold Michael Kors chronograph on his wrist looked nice, though it probably wasn't too expensive. His entire outfit could be purchased at any Nordstrom store, but this guy probably got it all at an outlet mall. Even more likely, his wife got it there. Though he wasn't wearing a wedding ring, the white line on his ring finger indicated he usually wore one while golfing in the California sunshine.

Her drink empty, she pushed it away and said, "I'd love to live near a sunny beach."

Steven nodded, then took a look around the bar. "Let's grab a table. What d'you say?"

Before she could answer, Steven flagged down the bartender, told him to put her drinks on his tab, and ordered a second round.

* * * *

Steven grabbed his drink—a single malt scotch on the rocks—and stood up to search for a table, ultimately selecting a booth along the wall.

He motioned for her to sit. She set her bag in the corner, tucked her dress, and scooted across the leather-like surface.

He scooted in next to her, instead of taking one of the open chairs across the table. Steven's game was improving, and that brought a slight smile to her face.

They talked about hometowns—how she's originally from Virginia and how he's always lived in California. They talked about travel, how flying places used to be kind of fun. She told him she managed a small boutique, and how it doesn't pay well, but she gets a great discount on awesome clothes. He talked about his consulting work with companies all over the country.

By the third round of drinks, Steven had gotten pretty handsy, comfortably resting his palm on her thigh as they talked about how both of them had flights tomorrow. He hadn't asked yet, but he was definitely interested in taking things upstairs to his room. In his mind, it was the only possible outcome of this chance encounter—they're both in town tonight, neither have anywhere to go until tomorrow—so sex was the obvious thing to fill the time in between.

She expected him to make a move, or at least hint at going to his room, but then he began telling a story about how the last time he was in town it was during a major convention, and he had to book a hotel almost an hour away to even get a room.

Jess wasn't really listening though. She was distracted by the woman at the table across from them. She'd just arrived, and she was talking loudly on her phone, clearly upset about something.

Steven noticed too, and soon his eyes also shifted to the woman. After a moment, he said, "What's going on?"

Jess shook her head. "I don't know. She seems really upset."

The woman was gorgeous and young, around twenty five. Her skin olive and perfect, her long brown hair draped across her delicate shoulders as if it had been painted there.

Her outfit was as stunning as she was—expensive designer jeans, a simple V-neck tee with a black blazer over it. The tee was probably two hundred dollars; the jeans at least five hundred. But the real eye-catcher was the Francesco Russo ankle strap pumps on her feet. They had to set her back at least eight hundred.

Jess and Steven watched her as she collapsed into a chair, tossing a leather Louboutin tote bag on the table, its signature red bottom adding one more pop of color to the trendy bar.

With one elbow on the table, the woman rested her head on her hand as she said, "I don't know what I'm going to do. I can't change my flight at this point."

She spoke with a British accent, her voice soft and soothing to the ears, even though she was in distress.

Finishing her phone call, she rested her head on both hands looking as though she might cry.

Jess spoke loudly across the table, "Excuse me. Are you all right?"

The woman didn't respond for a moment, but then she turned to look their way, wearing a look of surprise that a stranger was interested in her problems. She nodded and said, "Oh, yes. Thank you." Her accent made her more intriguing, and her stunning green eyes almost seemed backlit.

Steven stared at her for a moment, then returned his attention to Jess and restarted his story.

The woman stood and came to their table. Interrupting Steven, she said, "Actually, things aren't going so well. I don't suppose either of you would be keen on buying a bag or wallet, would you? It's excellent stuff, really. Designer stuff. Saint Laurent. I've got a shoulder bag and a beautiful, pebbled calfskin wallet I need to sell."

Jess glanced at Steven, then returned her attention to the woman standing at their table, "Why are you selling them?"

"I'm afraid it's quite a story, really. You see, it's my job. I'm a sales rep for a luxury retailer in London. I'm in the States to meet some buyers—in fact, I was supposed to meet one just now, but they've gone and canceled on me. So now, I'm stuck with these bags—which I've paid nearly seventeen hundred US for."

She grabbed the tote bag off the table and pulled the shoulder bag and wallet out for them to see. "My flight leaves tonight, and I can't get on the plane with these. If I take them back to London with me, I'll have to pay import duties. I can't say how much that'll be exactly, but it would be phenomenal, I'm sure."

Steven shook his head. "I'm sorry, but we're not interested."

The woman's shoulders slumped. "Are you certain? If you'd buy these from me for seventeen hundred dollars, you could list them on eBay for twice that much, easily. They'd sell in a matter of hours. I'd do it myself if I didn't have a flight to catch."

Steven went quiet. He seemed to be thinking about it. "Twice that amount?"

The woman nodded and said, "Without a doubt."

Steven's hand slid from Jess's leg and into his pocket. Under the table, out of the woman's view, he checked the amount of cash he had, then said, "They're really worth that much?"

The woman nodded. "Most definitely." Sliding into the booth next to Steven, she laid the merchandise on the table in front of him. Holding up the shoulder bag, she said, "This one here. It retails for twenty three hundred dollars."

Steven took the bag and examined it closely.

The woman held up the wallet and said, "This here, this one retails for about eleven hundred."

Steven set the shoulder bag on the table and took the wallet from her. He opened the flap, then traced the edges with the pad of his thumb.

The woman leaned over, making eye contact with Jess. She said, "I'm sorry. I'm afraid I've been quite rude. My name is Chloe."

Jess introduced herself, Steven too. He stared at the goods, his mind likely busy thinking about the potential profit. Then he said, "I can give you eight hundred."

Chloe gasped slightly then said, "For both?"

Steven nodded.

"I'm afraid I can't do that." Chloe took the bags back, then stood up. "That's a bigger loss than the duties I'd have to pay. I'm sorry. And I'm sorry to have bothered you. Thank you both for your time."

Chloe fumbled to get the bag and wallet back into the tote bag, and Steven said, "Hold on." He patted the booth next to him where she'd been seated. "Please, stay. We'll get some drinks, and we'll see if we can work out a price that works for both of us."

Chloe smiled, then sat beside Steven. Within seconds his other hand found its way to Chloe's thigh. His full attention shifted to her as well, as though Jess were no longer sitting on the other side of him.

* * * *

Steven caught the attention of a waitress and ordered himself a beer as Chloe checked out the wine selections. Looking up from the menu, she said, "I'll have a glass of the Merry Edwards pinot noir, please."

Jess nodded in agreement. "That sounds perfect. I'll have the same."

Steven's hand was back on Jess's leg, his other arm thrown over the back of the booth ensuring it was out of the way so Chloe could get as close as she'd like.

They'd stopped talking about Yves Saint Laurent accessories. He was now peppering Chloe with questions about London. He'd never been, but maybe she could show him around someday. She laughed, scooted closer, and agreed.

Steven squeezed Jess's thigh, turned his head toward her and said, "Maybe she could show both of us around, right?"

Jess smiled and said, "Now that could be fun."

Steven smiled a big grin.

He seemed in no hurry to work out a deal on the bag and wallet. He wanted to know more about Chloe. Where in England she'd grown up. What she did in her spare time. And he acted shocked when she said she didn't have a boyfriend.

"I travel a lot for work," she said. "Haven't got the time, I guess."

Steven nodded an understanding nod, then said, "I know what that's like. I feel like I'm in a different city every day."

Their drinks arrived and Steven settled deeper into the padded booth, now wrapping his other arm around Jess's shoulders. The three chatted, and Steven laughed loudly at things that weren't funny, an obvious ploy to gain the attention of the other patrons who'd begun filing into the bar at the end of the workday. This was clearly the highest point in his life—drinking in a fancy bar with two young, beautiful women at his side. He wanted everyone to notice.

* * * *

Steven ordered another round of drinks. He wiped beer from his mouth and said, "All right then, let's see what we can work out for these bags."

Chloe had brought it up at least twice during the second round of drinks, but Steven was clearly relishing the time with both of them and hadn't wanted to discuss matters of money. But as they waited for another round of drinks to come, it seemed he welcomed the conversation to fill the time between beers.

Steven picked the YSL wallet up and examined it. "You really need seventeen hundred bucks for these, huh?"

Chloe nodded and said, "That's my cost. I'd really like to break even, you know? Like I said, you'd be able to get a lot more for them."

"How do I know these aren't fakes? I mean, I'm not accusing you of anything, but I have to admit, I don't know shit about things like this." He laughed, loudly. "These could have come from Walmart, and I'd never know the difference." Another loud laugh.

Chloe took the wallet from him, folded back the flap, and said, "Look inside. Each one's got a serial number, and the style number. You can look that up on their website."

He examined it closely and said, "Made in Italy, huh." He thought for a moment and then said, "But still, that stuff's easy to fake, right?"

Jess decided to speak up. "Look at the stitching."

He looked at her, his eyebrows raised with surprise. "Oh yeah? What about it?"

She took the wallet from him and ran her finger across the side. "The stitching on this is very straight. Counterfeiters don't put that kind of effort in."

Steven took the wallet and examined the stitching closely. "Yeah, that is straight."

Jess nodded, then picked up the shoulder bag. "The leather is high quality too. Look at the sheen. It's real, and it's a great quality leather. Again, counterfeiters don't use quality materials like this."

Steven nodded as he took the bag from her. He looked at it briefly before saying to Chloe, "Jess knows this stuff pretty good. She sells this kind of stuff."

Chloe leaned into the table to speak to Jess, "Oh yeah? Are you in the industry?"

Jess nodded and said, "I run a boutique. We sell lots of luxury items."

"Fabulous." Chloe smiled. "Then this is perfect. If you have any trouble selling these online, perhaps you could sell them in your store? You could surely get the full retail price there."

Steven seemed happy about the prospect. He turned to Jess and said, "That could work. What d'you think? It'd give me a reason to come visit you in Maine."

She smiled and said, "I could sell them fast."

"You think you can get the full price?"

Jess took the handbag and looked inside, then checked out the wallet. "How much did you say they're worth?"

Chloe leaned in again and said, "Twenty three hundred for the bag, and eleven hundred for the chained wallet."

Steven had his phone out, already looking them up online. He clicked a few links and then said, "She's not kidding. I had no idea these things were so expensive."

Jess set them both on the table and slid them toward Chloe. She turned to Steven and said, "I know two or three customers who'd want these. I might even be able to call them in the morning and arrange a sale through the phone."

Steven reached into his pocket and pulled out the wad of cash again. Counting out the bills, he placed them on the table in front of him. "I've got eight hundred on me. Well, that and seven in singles." He turned to Jess. "Sorry to ask, sweetie, but do you have anything on you?"

Jess reached into her bag and retrieved her wallet. She dug out the cash inside and set it on the table. "Twenty bucks. That's all I've got."

Chloe sighed, then slid the YSL bags back into her tote. "Well, thank you both very much. I'm afraid I just can't sell them for that amount. I quite appreciate your time though."

Jess placed her hand on Steven's leg and said, "What about an ATM? There's probably one in the hotel lobby."

Steven thought about it for a moment, then said, "Okay. Let's go see, shall we, sweetie?"

Jess nodded.

Chloe stood so they could get out of the booth.

Jess slid out and stood beside Steven. He leaned into Chloe and said, "We'll hit the ATM. Why don't you flag that waitress down and get us some more drinks."

* * * *

They walked in silence until they were across the lobby. At the ATM, Steven looked across the room toward the bar. Secure in the idea that Chloe couldn't hear him, he said, "You're sure those are the real deal?"

Jess nodded and said, "Definitely. The leather is great quality, and the stitching too. The logos are nicely centered and clean. That's never the case with fakes. Honestly, if they're fakes, then they're the best I've ever seen. And if that's the case, my customers won't know either."

He thought it over briefly and then said, "So, you're sure we can get the full thirty four hundred for them?"

"At least close to it. Three grand, for sure."

"How quickly could you sell 'em?"

"By the end of the week, for sure. Probably a lot quicker though. A few of my regular customers love stuff like that. I can make a few phone calls tomorrow, and I may even have them sold before the end of the day."

"People are that crazy for this stuff, huh?"

Jess shrugged. "What can I say? Girls like pretty things."

His hands on his hips, Steven thought about it, then turned to the ATM and slid his card into the slot. After a few beeps, the machine spit out several bills. Steven took a quick count then said, "I've got an idea."

He'd piqued her interest for sure. "What kind of an idea?"

"If we pay her seventeen hundred, then sell them for three grand, that's a profit of thirteen hundred, which is not a bad profit at all."

"Seems good to me."

He nodded and said, "But she seems desperate to sell these things. That puts us in a good position to get a better deal." He held up the wad of cash. "I only pulled out five hundred. That's a total of thirteen hundred bucks. I'm thinking we tell her that my bank limited me to five hundred. If she thinks all we've got is thirteen hundred, she'll take it. Thirteen hundred seems like a fair price to me."

Jess nodded in agreement. "I guess so, but what if she walks away altogether?"

"I don't think she will." He began to walk back to the bar.

She grabbed his arm and said, "Wait."

Steven turned to face her, his face covered in confusion.

Jess stroked his arm and said, "I have a backup plan. Pull out another four hundred. I'll hang onto it, and if she won't take our deal, then I'll get up and pretend to go to the ATM. She doesn't know I don't have a debit card."

Steven thought it over, staring off toward the entrance. Finally, he said, "Okay, yeah. That's smart."

* * * *

Chloe was sipping a glass of brandy when they returned to the table. A matching glass awaited Jess, and another scotch on the rocks sat for Steven. In the center of the table, three shot glasses filled with something awaited them.

Jess sat down in one of the chairs and took a sip of brandy. It was quality, for sure. Chloe definitely knew her booze.

Chloe was happy. Smiling. Certain she was about to get her money and be on her way. She laughed, and giggled, then pulled Steven down into the booth to sit beside her.

Chloe grabbed one of the shot glasses and said, "Let's celebrate, yes?"

Steven looked sad. He rubbed Chloe's thigh and said, "Sorry. Um, the ATM machine limited me to five hundred." He pulled the cash from his pocket and set it on the table. "The best I can do is thirteen hundred."

Chloe sipped her drink as she thought it over. "There's no way you can get the other four hundred? Can you call your bank or something?"

"Sorry. I tried. They said they can't change the limit for twenty four hours. Some kind of security safeguard, I guess."

A wave of respect for Steven washed over Jess. He was much quicker on his feet than she'd given him credit for.

Chloe looked at Jess. "How about you? Is there any way you can make up the difference?"

Before she could answer, Steven said, "I'm sorry. I'd really love to help you out, but I'm afraid thirteen is the best we can do."

Jess sipped her brandy as Chloe contemplated the cash that was literally on the table.

Chloe finished the last drink of her brandy, patted Steven's hand, then stood up. "Well, thank you for trying." Grabbing her gorgeous Louboutin tote, she flung the strap over her shoulder and said, "I really need the full amount, and I'd better get going. I can't miss my flight."

Jess finished the brandy and said, "Chloe, wait." She grabbed her bag off the table. "Let me go to the ATM. I'll see if I can make up the difference."

"Yeah?" A wide smile filled Chloe's youthful face. "I quite appreciate that."

Jess walked out of the bar and into the lobby. Once she was around the corner, she leaned against the wall and retrieved her phone from her bag. No one had called or messaged. She scrolled through Facebook a little. Nothing too new. Her friend Monica got a new puppy. Emily's little girl was walking now, apparently.

Jess dropped her phone back into her bag and retrieved the cash Steven had given her.

Walking back into the bar, she found Steven nestled up close to Chloe. Again, he laughed loudly.

Jess held the cash up so Chloe could see it. "Four hundred. That gives you the full seventeen hundred."

Chloe stood up and hugged Jess. "Thank you so much, love. Oh, I can't tell you how great you both are." Chloe grabbed the stack of cash Steven had set on the table, then took the cash from Jess's hand.

Chloe finished counting the money, then produced a small Manila envelope from her tote bag. She slid the cash inside the envelope, then slid the envelope into the inside pocket of her blazer. "This is cause for celebration, yes?" She motioned toward the shots on the table. "I took the liberty of ordering us tequila. I hope that's okay."

Steven pulled her onto the bench seat, almost into his lap. "That's perfect." He picked up one of the shots, held it into the air and said, "To Chloe. May she have a safe trip back to London."

They all raised their shots, then tossed them back. It had a smooth taste, especially for tequila.

Chloe stood again, picked up the tote bag and said, "I guess these are yours now." She reached in and began to pull the YSL bags out, then paused. "Unless…" She thought for a moment. "Yes, I can't believe I didn't think about this earlier. I've got two other bags up in my room. Maybe you'd like those better? One's a Louis Vuitton. I could swap that one for the wallet, maybe. Since you're helping me out so much. It's worth quite a bit more than the wallet. You'd make a bigger profit."

Steven shook his head. Before he could speak, Jess said, "I wouldn't mind seeing the Louis Vuitton, for sure."

She felt Steven shooting her a look, but she ignored him, keeping her focus on Chloe, who said, "Yeah? Okay, let me go grab it real quick." She began to walk away, but Jess stopped her.

"Wait. You're not taking our cash *and* the bags, are you?"

"Oh, my." Chloe reached into her jacket pocket and pulled out the envelope. "I wasn't thinking. My apologies." She set the envelope on the table. "I'll leave that right there. I'll only be a few moments."

Steven stood. "I'll go with you."

Chloe stepped close to him, her face inches from his. "I'm sorry, love. I don't let men into my room. You can understand, can't you?"

Steven nearly smiled, despite being turned down, seemingly intoxicated by her flirting.

Jess interrupted and said, "I'll go with you then."

Chloe turned toward her. "Oh, okay. Sure thing, love."

Jess grabbed her bag and said, "I'm sorry. I don't mean to imply that you're some kind of con artist or something, but we did just meet you."

"No offense taken." Chloe smiled. "Shall we, then?" Jess glanced at Steven. He nodded slightly, then patted the envelope on the table. She nodded at Chloe and said, "Okay. Let's see this Louis Vuitton."

Steven sipped his scotch as the two walked out of the bar. In the lobby, Chloe laughed and said, "Don't you think the con artist line was a bit much?"

Jess chuckled. "I thought it was funny."

"It was a bit much." Chloe's British accent was gone.

"You're dropping the accent already?"

"You like that, do you?"

"It has a certain appeal."

Chloe smiled, and with the accent she said, "Sure thing, governor."

As they walked out though the big sliding doors to the parking lot, Jess gave a look over her shoulder. It seemed Steven was a good boy and had stayed like he'd been told. The waitress should be bringing his bill around soon, which would be a shock.

As they approached the car, Jess said, "How much was that brandy?"

Chloe laughed. "Technically, it was cognac. Remy Martin X.O. Thirty six bucks a glass."

"I see why. It was damn good." She tossed her bag in the back seat. "And the tequila?"

"Don Julio Real. I think that one was sixty five per shot. Hell, the pinot was twenty five a glass, and we had, what? Six of those between us. Plus, I'm guessing he picked up your initial drinks. Virgin mojito, I assume?"

"Three of them."

Chloe rolled her eyes. "Virgin though?"

"Got to keep my wits about me. What if I were to get drunk and run off with the guy?"

Chloe laughed, then said, "Oh, shit." She set the tote bag on the roof. "I almost forgot." She produced a bottle of wine from the bag.

"Where'd that come from?"

"I ordered it when you two went to the ATM. I told them we were going to drink it in the room, so we didn't need glasses. Waitress thought nothing of it when I put it in my bag."

Jess smiled. "Nice touch."

Chloe inspected it. "Chambolle-Musigny. It's a twenty twelve."

"What'd that set him back?"

"Two forty, I think?"

Chloe reached into her pocket, grabbed the envelope, then tossed it to Jess. "You want to look after that for us?"

After draping her blazer over the back of the driver's seat, Chloe sat down and started the car. Jess sat in the passenger seat and took a look at the cash. By now, Steven was surely growing impatient with how long they'd been gone. In their absence, he'd finish his drink. He'd eventually look at the envelope on the table, poke at it with his thick fingers, spin it on the table in front of him.

He'd look toward the bar entrance, wondering what's taking them so damn long (women, right?). He'd poke at the envelope some more until curiosity and suspicion took over and forced him to open it.

Plunging his fingers inside, he'd pull out the contents. His jaw would drop as he realized there's no cash inside, just a stack of neatly trimmed clippings from an old *Vogue* magazine. He'd slam the envelope on the table as he wondered how, and when, Chloe made the switch.

Jess smiled to herself as she pictured it. Leaning over, she kissed Chloe on the cheek. "Thanks for a fun night."

"Anytime." Chloe smiled as she exited the parking lot and drove away from the hotel.

Jess watched the city pass by them out the car window. About now, Steven was probably trying to figure out what happened. Replaying the entire evening, realizing Jess was in on it all along, and wondering how he let it happen.

The worst part wasn't even over for him. He'd settle the bar tab, somehow. He'd eventually get over the loss of seventeen hundred dollars in cash. But what he probably hadn't thought about yet was his wife. How long would it be until she learned about the credit card charges, or the ATM withdrawals? A couple grand spent on a few hours in a hotel bar with two beautiful girls he never had a shot with. To a guy like Steven, that probably seemed like a fair price.

R.M. Lowery is the author of the Jakob Larsen Mysteries—*The Gentle Slope, We Kill Our Own*, and *Time Doesn't Wait*. His stories have appeared in *Workers Write: Tales from the Key of C, Tradiciones*, and elsewhere. Rooted in Illinois and raised in Colorado, Lowery currently lives in New Mexico with his beautiful wife and their clowder of cats. Learn more at rmlowery.com.

THE CHILD

ELIZABETH ELWOOD

I will never forget the child. Those wide blue eyes that had seen such terrible things will haunt me to the end of my days, and I daily give thanks for my own children with their happy dispositions and secure, uncomplicated lives. May they never know the darkness that exists in the parallel, less-ordered universes all around us.

The Houghton murders happened early in my career. The child was Talia Houghton, the little girl who survived. I was a young lawyer, still articling and earning income from legal aid. As such, I was assigned to defend Danny Houghton, the man first charged with the shooting. Never have I had a client I disliked more. He was a nasty piece of work, a tall, muscular brute with black hair and startling blue eyes, which, when you looked into them, stared back at you like stagnant pools. No life, no empathy, no feeling rose from those impervious depths. He was as predatory as the cougar tattooed on his back, and clever and cunning as well. A classic psychopath, he was adept at dodging drug convictions and evading assault charges, the latter because his victims were too scared to bear witness against him. The charges he now faced were two counts of murder and one of attempted murder. All three victims were children. Talia, the one who survived, was his own daughter.

I can still see that child, a fragile waif besieged by tubes and wires, so frailly linked to life that one felt compelled to hold one's breath in her presence for fear that an outrush of air would blow her away into the ether. Later, when she came round, I see her as a tiny wraith, dwarfed by her hospital bed, but bravely focusing those bright blue eyes and trying so hard to answer the questions of the investigating officer. Later, in court, the courage of this seven-year-old brought tears to the eyes of all present as she dutifully, tragically described what had happened that terrible night. A tiny blond miracle of survival, traumatized by her past, but finally, I prayed, with hope for the future.

Still, that came later. When I was first assigned to defend Danny, I knew nothing of his family, but I was appalled when I learned the history behind the case. As I read about the home life of these children, I realized I was light years from comprehending the mindset of their parents. How could anyone be so indifferent to the needs of the babes they had brought into the world?

Danny's ex-wife, Lara, lived in a ramshackle camper in a trailer court in the Cariboo. She had borne him a daughter named Talia in December of

1999, but after three months, Danny walked out on her. Lara, if not a psychopath like her husband, was definitely a sociopath, preferring to go out and party rather than care for her children. Two more children were fathered by her next boyfriend, Johnny Robbins, who moved in as soon as Danny left, but he, too, moved on soon after his second child was born. In his case, the move was not voluntary, because he had been sentenced to twelve years for armed robbery. Lara was in and out of rehab—when in, her children were cared for by Denise Brooks, a friend who lived nearby; when out, Talia became caregiver for the younger two.

Lara seemed indifferent to the way her drug and alcohol use affected the children's lives, not to mention what they suffered from the men she hitched up with along the way. Danny Houghton drifted in and out of her life between her multiple boyfriends, although at the time of the murders, she was living with Brad Jakes, a loutish and aggressive truck driver with the same propensity for violence as Danny. The children ran wild from the moment they were old enough to walk, and by the time Talia was seven, she was a familiar figure to local residents, for she trekked about with five-year-old Bobby and four-year-old Sue in tow, cadging candy at the local store and hunting for miscellaneous treasures lost or abandoned by tourists at the lakeshore.

In the summer of 2007, the ragtag trio came to the attention of a middle-aged couple who owned a cottage by the lake. Marion and Brian Graham had never had children, much to their regret, and Marion's heart went out to the three waifs who daily patrolled the shoreline. It took very little time before she befriended them, and soon the children were regular visitors at the cottage, enjoying healthy treats that they had never known existed, having been raised on a diet of frozen pizza, processed macaroni dinners and whatever tinned fare was available from the food bank.

It wasn't long before Marion Graham became vocal about the children's living conditions and their lack of parental care. This caused friction between Lara and Brad, the latter already resenting the children and determined that they would not cause him any trouble. On Canada Day, things came to a head. Marion Graham entered the general store to find the manager threatening the children with the police if he ever again caught them helping themselves to the merchandise. Marion paid for the goods, took charge of the children, and brought them home. Her fury was sufficiently unrestrained that several residents, including Annie Marks, the elderly woman in the adjacent trailer, witnessed the tirade she delivered to the children's mother. After Marian left, Brad raged at Lara, threatened the children, and then stormed off to the pub. Lara was angry, too, and she went out, having decreed that the children's punishment was to miss going to town to see the fireworks. She finally returned at eleven o'clock. Shortly afterwards, Annie Marks was awoken by the sound of screaming. Lara was crying that someone had shot her children.

Bobby and Sue were both dead, but Talia was still alive, and she was rushed to hospital where she remained in a coma for the next three weeks. In the meantime, the police found the gun in Lara's trailer. It was a Remington 870 twelve-gauge shotgun. The serial number had been filed off and there were no fingerprints. The weapon had been wiped clean. Lara insisted that she had no idea where the gun had come from or who had carried out the shootings. She told the police that she had spent the evening with Denise Brooks and had only discovered the carnage when she returned to her trailer.

The investigating officer was convinced that Lara was lying, not about her whereabouts, for Denise backed up her story, but about her knowledge of the shooter. He was also sure she recognized the gun. It was entirely possible that she was covering up for her current partner, either through fear, or simply because she didn't want to lose her means of support. Annie Marks had been outside earlier that day and had overheard Brad yelling at the children. She told the police that he'd laid his fists on them in the past and had threatened to walk out if Lara didn't stop them causing trouble. Lara, she added, was no better. She never stood up for the children and seemed more interested in mollifying her mate than protecting her offspring from his bullying. However, Annie Marks had not seen anyone entering or leaving Lara's trailer—the entrance, pointing outward to the perimeter of the property, was screened from view—and, having noticed the local teenagers preparing for an evening of fireworks, she had gone to bed fortified with earplugs to block the anticipated noise. Yes, she had been woken up a couple of times by the explosions but had not looked at the clock and had simply drifted off again.

There were no other witnesses. Annie Mark's trailer, like Lara's, was located in a remote corner and divided from the rest of the court by a row of cedars, so no one could see anything that happened in their enclave. Neither were there clues to the timing of the shots since the teenagers had only stopped setting off firecrackers when they heard the screams coming from Lara's trailer.

In spite of Brad being the obvious suspect, his alibi proved unassailable. His visit to the pub had lasted from four in the afternoon until closing time and had been witnessed by a huge crowd of people. It had been Saturday night, and the place was packed. His car had been blocked in by the later arrivals and he had not been able to get it out until the bar closed at midnight. Once Brad was eliminated, the other men in Lara's life came under scrutiny. Johnny Robbins was easily cleared since he was still doing time, but Danny Houghton was definitely in the frame. He had also showed up at the pub that night, but not until quarter to ten. He lived in a rented cottage on a thickly forested property adjacent to the trailer park.

When one of Danny's associates let slip the fact that he'd seen him use a Remington 870 for hunting, Danny was brought in for questioning. Danny insisted that he owned a Winchester 12-guage and that Lara had inherited the Remington from her old man. Danny had used it when he lived with her but left it behind when he moved out. He said Lara was lying because she didn't have a firearms license and because she knew that Johnny Robbins had used the shotgun during the robbery. Johnny was the one who had filed off the serial number.

However, Johnny denied any knowledge of the gun and Lara continued to back him up. The police had been itching to nail Danny for years and now they had a chance to make a charge stick. Word had leaked out that he was angry about Lara's demands for money, and in the eyes of the local constabulary, he was as capable of snuffing out an inconvenient daughter as he would be of swatting a mosquito. As a result, Johnny Robbin's statement was believed, and Danny was charged with the murders.

In spite of Danny's surly assertion that he was being set up by his bitch ex-wife who had learned to shoot at her father's knee, I was convinced of my client's guilt. Therefore, I was unconcerned when my indifferent efforts to get him out on bail met with failure. However, the shocking events that followed jarred me out of my complacency. Either through deliberate negligence from the guards, or malicious contrivance from the prisoners who had witnessed Johnny Robbins's agony at learning the fate of his children, Danny was stabbed to death in his prison cell.

Soon afterwards, Lara's alibi disintegrated. On the night of the murders, Denise Brook's husband had come home early enough to realize that Lara's story could not be true. Under pressure from him, Denise came clean. Lara had not been with her that night. She had gone to see Danny. She had asked Denise to cover for her because she'd been afraid of Brad finding out where she had been.

Caught in the lie, Lara admitted that she'd been at Danny's cottage. She'd gone there because she wanted more money for Talia's care. In the course of the visit, they'd started drinking, one thing led to another, and they ended up in bed. She had dozed off, and when she woke up, Danny had disappeared. She was angry, because he'd promised to help her, and once again, he'd taken advantage of her and let her down. She'd had a couple more drinks and waited around, hoping he'd come back, but had finally given up, got dressed and staggered home, only to discover the terrible fate of her children.

This story had the ring of truth, but when the forensic report came in, Lara was caught in a much more serious lie. X-ray technology had identified the serial number on the shotgun and the police had traced the original owner. Danny had been right. The gun had belonged to Lara's father. A second, more thorough search of the trailer uncovered boxes of ammunition in a paneled-in enclosure under the bed.

Now a chilling possibility presented itself. It had happened before that a woman had killed her children to prevent a man from walking out on her. Lara Houghton was a drug addict, an alcoholic, clearly unstable, and judging by the lack of care her children received, an indifferent and resentful mother. The debris in Danny's cottage that night had indicated drug use as well as overindulgence in alcohol. Could Lara have returned in a psychotic state brought on by substance abuse and obliterated her children in a frenzy of rage and frustration?

And when Talia Houghton recovered from her wounds, she confirmed that disturbing truth. It had been her mother who had fired the deadly shots. Faced with the child's testimony, Lara collapsed. When her hysterical sobbing subsided, she acknowledged her guilt and seemed resigned to accepting her fate. In spite of her remorse and her plea of temporary insanity, the judge at her trial issued a twenty-five-year sentence with no chance of parole until twelve years had been served.

Who was to realize what havoc would be let loose when that period finally elapsed?

* * * *

After Danny's death, I was finished with the Houghton case, for another lawyer was assigned to handle Lara's defense. However, I was concerned about the child and visited her regularly during her time in hospital. Virtually orphaned, with her only living parent in police custody, she had been treated with loving care by the nursing staff, but her greatest solace came from the Grahams. They were a constant presence, reassuring her, encouraging her to heal, and promising her a better future. I had been pleased to hear that they intended to adopt Talia, but after that happy piece of news, I lost touch and become immersed in other work.

Ten years passed before I heard of Talia again. I was no longer a trainee scraping by on legal aid, but a successful lawyer with one of Vancouver's most reputable firms. I owned a house on acreage in the Fraser Valley where I lived with my talented stage-designer wife and two lovely children. That particular day, Sandra was in town for a meeting at the Arts Club, so we met up for dinner after she was through. As we were enjoying coffee and dessert, I suddenly sensed we were being watched. I looked up to see a middle-aged couple staring at us from a table by the window. There was something familiar about the pair, especially the woman with her neatly styled hair and plain, navy wool dress. When I caught her eye, she stood up, spoke briefly with her husband, pulled an iPhone from her purse, and came over to our table. I could tell from her purposeful stride that she knew who I was, but I could not place her until she introduced herself. It was Marion Graham.

"It is Craig Treadwell, isn't it?" she said. "I was sure I recognized you. We've always remembered how kind you were to Talia."

I introduced her to Sandra, who had read about the murders at the time of Lara's trial and had been fascinated, when first we met, to hear that I had been Danny Houghton's lawyer. Then I inquired after Talia.

"How is she doing?" I asked.

"Graduated from Grade 12 with honors and hoping for a future in law. She's also a great little actress and starred in her high-school production of *Grease*." Marion Graham set her phone on the table. The screen displayed a vibrant young woman in cap and gown, with tawny golden hair spilling out from under her mortarboard. Vitality radiated from her beautiful smile and those bright blue eyes…and yet something else was in those eyes. I couldn't read what it was, but it made me uneasy. I looked up and raised my eyebrows.

"No lingering issues?" I asked.

Our visitor's expression became grave.

"Yes, of course there are. You can't erase her past. For years she had terrible nightmares, and she's still afraid of her mother. She knows she's safe with us, but trauma-induced fears don't have to be rational. Still, her progress has been amazing. She's studying hard and enjoying all the fun that goes with college life. We sold our North Shore house and bought a townhouse in Kitsilano as it's closer for her to commute, but we have a cottage on the Sunshine Coast—we couldn't keep the Cariboo property after what happened there—and Talia loves spending summers by the ocean. She's a wonderful daughter and we're lucky to have her."

"She was lucky to have found you," I said. "You changed the path of life for that little girl."

Marian Graham smiled grimly.

"Yes, it was an ascent from Hell to Heaven," she said. "If only we could eradicate her past, everything would be perfect."

I was to remember those words two years later. We had come through a cold winter, with icy landscapes and frigid temperatures severe enough to chill any cheerful thoughts into oblivion, but now, at the end of March, the first signs of spring were emerging. I was on my way to work, having left early to get ahead of rush-hour traffic. The world was still dark: the shadowy vacuum on my right concealed a silent and invisible river and the rock face on my left obscured all signs of habitation. The pitch-black sky hung like a shroud, only penetrated by the intermittent flash of headlights and a few glittering towers in the distance. I had switched on the news to get the traffic report, but the broadcast was interrupted as a call came through from George Brock, the head of my law firm. He wasted no time with preliminaries.

"Remember Talia Houghton, the child in that shooting case when you were starting out? She needs a lawyer and her parents have asked that you represent her."

I was momentarily stunned into silence. I rounded a corner, and the soaring silver and gold arches of the Port Mann Bridge came into view. The glimmering arcs swept across the sky like a giant monitor, and suddenly I was back in the hospital room, watching the helpless figure in the bed, aching with grief for the child whose eyes seemed to plead with me to make her well, to make all things well in a situation where nothing might ever be well again. The concrete stanchions of the bridge drew near, the arches loomed overhead, and my car swept into the dark hollow under the bridge deck. Inside the void, I finally found my voice.

"Why does she need a lawyer?" I asked.

"She's killed her mother," he replied.

* * * *

As soon as I arrived downtown, I picked up a coffee from Starbucks—necessary fortification, given the shock of George's phone call—and took it up to my office. I was determined to take on Talia's defense with all the passion that had been lacking when I had been given the dispiriting task of defending her father. George was waiting to brief me.

"Hopefully, she'll only face a manslaughter charge," he said, "but it could be second-degree murder. It's a grisly killing. Lara was battered to death with a ten-pound exercise weight."

"Where did it happen?"

"At the Grahams' townhouse."

"Is there any room for doubt? Are we sure Talia was the killer?"

"Oh, yes. Talia has admitted it. Besides, there's a witness. A young man was walking along the street with his girlfriend and heard cries for help coming from inside the townhouse. The patio door was open, so while his girlfriend called the police, he vaulted the terrace wall and ran inside to help. By the time he got there, Lara was inert and bleeding on the floor. Talia was standing over her. The exercise weight lay on the floor beside the body and the room showed signs of a struggle. An end table had been knocked over. Magazines littered the floor, and a tall bud vase lay broken by the chesterfield. A daffodil lay nearby on a wet patch on the carpet. Talia had a red mark on her cheek and her face was puffing up and swollen, so something had definitely struck her, but it was minimal compared to the degree of violence done to her mother."

I shook my head and sighed.

"What was Lara doing at the townhouse? Had Talia agreed to see her?"

"No. I gather she simply showed up and came in through the patio doors. It's a ground-floor unit. The Grahams were away at their cottage, so Talia was on her own."

I shivered, remembering the wraith in the hospital bed and the vulnerability of that tiny little frame.

"She must have been in fear of her life."

"Yes, but whether that fear was justified or not is the question. Obviously, there was some kind of struggle, but other than sobbing that Lara was going to kill her, Talia hasn't made a formal statement. The Grahams have insisted that she see her lawyer prior to talking with the police."

"Sensible of them."

George nodded. "Yes, because it's going to be tricky. If Talia's perception of the threat from her mother was legitimate, then Lara did one hell of a job fooling the corrections system. This could become a case of Talia Houghton versus the parole board that gave her mother a 'get out of jail free' card. Paint Lara as a villain and you'll be challenging their success story. Read that," he added, handing me a Corrections Canada document.

I scanned the report quickly. It was a glowing endorsement. Lara was clean—no drug or alcohol abuse. She had undergone a religious conversion and had embraced the Roman Catholic faith. She had taken courses and was qualified to work as an esthetician. Her desire to see Talia and ask for forgiveness was sincere, but she would not push for a meeting unless her daughter was willing. The parole board was convinced that Lara's original crime was caused by substance abuse and toxic relationships and that she was now a completely different person from the irresponsible, abusive woman of her youth.

"See what I mean," said George when I set the paper down. "Model prisoner."

"How do you suggest we deal with it?" I asked.

"Well, if you want to make things easy, you can let politics prevail and cease worrying about what really happened. There's sympathy for Talia. No one disputes the fact that a rush of adrenalin produced by fear would explain her frenzied attack. The only dispute is whether or not her fear was justified. If you stick to the psychologist's assessment that her early trauma resulted in the *perception* that she had to defend herself and accept that the struggle that ensued came about because of her state of panic, the worst scenario would be a manslaughter conviction with a suspended sentence and requirements for counseling and ongoing psychiatric treatment. Any other approach might be difficult. There would have to be hard-core evidence of an attack."

"Then I'd better reserve judgment until I hear what Talia has to say."

By the time I got to interview Talia, the mark on her cheek had blossomed into a deep purple bruise that had spread up around her eye. Marian Graham was present, hovering over Talia like a brooding hen and eyeing me with an imperative stare that demanded I bring their adopted daughter through unscathed from her latest ordeal.

When I explained the approach that George had suggested, Talia seemed stunned into silence. Marian Graham, however, had lots to say.

"This is outrageous," she snapped. "Lara conned everyone into thinking she'd reformed, but her talk of reconciliation was a sham. Her letter was simply a cunning attempt to get at Talia."

"What letter?"

"It was forwarded from our lawyer. Lara asked for a meeting."

"When did this letter come?"

"Toward the end of September. It was the day after we received notice that Lara had reached the six-month period of day passes before her final release from jail.

I turned to Talia.

"How did you feel when you saw the letter?"

Talia bit her lip.

"Frightened," she said finally.

"Was there an implied threat in the letter?"

"No. It was polite enough. She sent me a phone number where I could reach her if I wanted to meet her. I was just scared at the idea of seeing her."

"So, you took no action?"

"I couldn't. I just wanted to forget it. I tried to put it from my mind."

Marian Graham broke in again.

"Yes, but soon afterward, she started receiving phone calls from an unidentified source. When she answered the calls, there was no one there, although she could hear someone breathing. It wasn't rocket science to figure out that Lara was responsible. That's why we applied for the restraining order."

"When did that come into effect?"

"Not until December, but things quieted down once it was in place. Life went back to normal. Talia was busy with school. She also had a part in her college musical so, come March, she was heavily tied up with rehearsals. Brian and I were spending spring break at the cottage, but Talia had to stay in town because of the show. We weren't concerned because the calls had stopped after the restraining order kicked in. We thought Lara had given up."

I turned back to Talia.

"What happened next?"

"Two days after her final release from jail, there was another call. I—" Talia paused and bit her lip again. Her eyes met mine and a question hovered in the air. "This time, I thought I heard her voice, but now I keep thinking I imagined it. I keep hearing the words, 'It's payback time,' but it could have just been in my head. I just don't know what to think. Was I wrong to be afraid of her? What if she did only want to see me to say she was sorry?" Talia broke off with a sob and sank down onto the sofa.

Marion Graham stared at me over her daughter's head.

"She keeps thinking she might have attacked Lara without cause, and we can't seem to get through to her that she was right to defend herself. That bruise on her face alone speaks volumes. The trouble is, she can't remember. It's all a big blank."

I sat down next to Talia and put my hand gently on her shoulder.

"Just tell me what you do remember, Talia. What did you do after you'd received the phone call?"

"I phoned Mom and Dad. They said they'd come back right away, but the trip takes four or five hours, so I was pretty frightened."

"We told her to stay home, keep the door locked, and wait until we arrived," Marion Graham interjected.

"Did you do that?" I asked Talia.

"Yes, but it was hard to concentrate on anything, so I just worked out on the patio. It's fenced in, so I felt safe there and I could see what was happening on the street."

"Why did you not see Lara coming?"

"I'd just finished working with the weights and had gone to get a glass of water from the kitchen."

"What had you done with the weights?"

"I put them down on the sofa."

"Then?"

"When I came back, I saw Lara standing inside the patio door."

"Did she speak to you? What did she say?"

Talia's bright eyes clouded.

"I can't remember. I don't think she said anything, but I can't be sure. I was so scared when I saw her that it was like I'd tuned out anything that wasn't already in my head. It was like watching a program when the sound goes out. I have this picture in my mind of the flowers spilling onto the floor. I can see Lara holding the vase. It was broken, and the jagged edge was in front of my face. I remember my hand falling against something hard and my fingers gripping it. It must have been the weight though I don't think I was conscious of it at the time. I just remember feeling that I had to strike out if I wasn't going to die."

Tears started to streak down Talia's cheeks. "I guess I kept on hitting her," she said sadly. "I just remember feeling that I had to stop her from ever hurting me again."

Talia remembered nothing more until she was standing with a stranger's arms around her, staring at the bloodied mess that remained of her mother. I hoped that the forensic evidence would provide some clarification, but in the meantime, I had a distressed girl on my hands and a police detective waiting to hear what she had to say. I took Talia in to make her official statement the following day.

Two weeks later, when the police report was complete, I was amazed to find evidence to indicate that Talia's perception of danger was not imagined. Lara's fingerprints were on the neck of the vase, and splinters of glass by the fireplace suggested that it had been smashed against the mantle. DNA on the base proved it had caused the injury to Talia's face, so it seemed likely that Lara had struck her daughter, then broken the vase and threatened her with the jagged edge. Talia must have fallen against the couch after the first blow, which was why, when she landed, her arm came to rest against the exercise weight. If, as she lay there, stunned, she saw her mother break the vase against the stone hearth of the fireplace, then raise her arm to strike again, it followed that she had gripped the weight, swung upwards and hit back.

The statement of the young man who had come to the rescue reinforced my conclusions. He was certain that it was Talia who had been calling for help. He had talked with her while they waited for the police and was confident in his identification of her voice. He'd distinctly heard her say, "Keep away from me!" and he was in no doubt that her distress was genuine.

The phone records also told a story. The call to Talia on the day of the incident was from Lara's cellphone, and the pay-as-you-go phone that had been used for the anonymous calls was found in her purse. Everything added up to a strong case for dismissal. However, there still remained the mystery as to *why* Lara had attacked her daughter. Had she really wanted to throw away her own future for one savage moment of revenge for Talia's childhood evidence? If so, how had she managed to cover her anger from the people in the corrections system?

By the time the case came to trial, we were no closer to answering those questions. Once the forensic evidence had been presented, Lara's parole officer acknowledged that the board had been mistaken in its judgment, but offered no explanation of what might have prompted the assault. Much of the weeklong trial was taken up with psychologists' reports regarding Talia's childhood and the effect of early trauma on her current state of mind, but Lara remained an enigma. It was a stressful week, and as it drew to a close, I could see that it had taken its toll on Talia. However, there had been no challenges to the evidence, and I was confident that the charges would be dismissed.

My wife was also anxious for a good result. Sandra was very interested in Talia's case, and she had got to know the Grahams well during the course of the investigation. She had accompanied me to the courthouse throughout the trial and had provided a great deal of moral support for Talia. On the final day, Sandra had an early production meeting downtown, but she arranged to meet me for lunch at the courthouse restaurant and then listen in on the afternoon session. As it happened, everything had wound up by noon and the jury was out by the time I went to join her. She was already seated when I arrived at the restaurant. As soon as I sat, she nodded toward a table in the corner. It was occupied by a gaunt woman with disheveled gray hair and protuberant eyes.

"Recognize her?"

"She looks familiar. Wasn't she was sitting in the courtroom during the trial?"

"Every day. She didn't miss a session. I was here early, so I picked up a coffee and, being nosy, invited myself to join her."

"So, who is she?"

"An ex-con who was in prison with Lara. She has a pretty amazing story to tell. She's the key to your mystery."

"What mystery?"

"The reason for the attack. This will blow your mind. She says it wasn't Lara who shot the children."

"What! She can't be serious."

"She certainly is. Her name's Marge Lonan, by the way. She didn't particularly like Lara. She said she was quiet and expressionless, with a brain fried from drink and drugs, and she hardly ever socialized with any of the other prisoners. She just kept to herself and did what she had to do to get through her sentence. But one day, the two of them were together on laundry duty and Lara unloaded on her. Johnny Robbins had been paroled the previous month and Marge was due for release, so Lara asked her to meet with Johnny and tell him that it really had been Danny who carried out the shootings."

"She was probably lying. With her parole coming up, she'd hardly want to be out in the world with Johnny loose and believing she'd killed his children, especially since he might have been the one who killed Danny for that very same reason. Besides, Lara confessed her guilt when she was arrested. How did the ex-con explain that?"

"Lara felt the shootings *were* her fault. If she hadn't pushed Danny for support, he would have left them alone. She was so upset, she didn't care what happened to her."

"Okay, but why not retract later when she got her head together?"

"Because she couldn't see how she'd be believed once Talia accused her, and then, later on, she realized that her only chance of ever being paroled was to continue to admit her guilt and let everyone see how sorry she was."

"Does her prison mate think Lara was out for revenge?"

"Yes, but she says she didn't realize it until she heard the details at the trial. At the time, she thought Lara simply wanted to let Talia know that she forgave her and that she understood why she had lied."

"*If* she lied. This is pretty far-fetched."

"Not really. Think about it. Lara was a rotten mother. She never stood up for her children. Talia must have dreaded being returned to her, and that's what would have happened if she'd told the police that Danny was the shooter. Besides, she had Marian Graham hanging about the hospital, aching to take her home, and promising her the moon. Can you blame Talia for making the choice that she did?"

* * * *

Between Sandra's bombshell, which I still didn't entirely believe, and the looming verdict for Talia, my lunch went down like lead. Feeling troubled and dyspeptic, I passed on dessert, left Sandra to finish hers alone, and went to join my clients in the courthouse. They were as anxious as I was, but our nerves proved unnecessary as the verdict from the sympathetic jury was just as I had predicted. The charges were dismissed, and Talia was free to go. Talia and her adoptive parents thanked me profusely and we said our farewells in the hall outside the courtroom.

Sandra had slipped into the back of the courtroom in time to hear the verdict and had joined me for my parting words with Talia and her parents. I was silent and preoccupied as we left the building, for suddenly it was over, but my stress had not lessened. I felt chilled, almost disoriented, and I only tuned in gradually to what my wife was saying as we walked back across the concourse.

"You know, the Grahams spoil that girl. They traded in a gorgeous West Vancouver home for a poky townhouse in Kits just so Talia would have an easy commute to school. And she has every designer label you can imagine hung on various parts of her anatomy, whereas Marion Graham, in case you hadn't noticed, is wearing a suit jacket that must date back to the nineties. Talia has them wrapped round her little finger."

"What brought that on?" I asked.

"I don't know. Yes, I do. I've been thinking about the story that Marge Conan told me. What if Lara really was telling the truth? Did she only want reconciliation with her daughter? What if the parole board had it right?"

"She attacked her daughter. The evidence was irrefutable."

"Yes, but I've been thinking about that too. Every incriminating detail could have been staged. Talia could have been the one using the pay-as-you-go phone to create 'anonymous' calls. She could have set up the meeting with her mother. She could have planted the phone in Lara's purse after the fact. The bruise could have been self-inflicted. The fingerprints on the vase could have been made by curling Lara's fingers around it after she was dead. Talia could have screamed for help *after* she'd staged the scene, knowing full well that someone would hear and appear as a witness. It could have been a premeditated scenario created by a girl who wanted to kill her mother."

"But why?" I asked. "What would she have to gain?"

"Stopping Lara from coming back into her life. Preventing her from telling the Grahams that she'd lied as a child in order to trade in her trailer-court lifestyle for upper middle-class comfort. Or maybe she really was scared that Lara was out for revenge. It's all pure theory, but any of those motives would be enough for a person who lacks the little edit button most of us have when it comes to moral behaviour. It would be interesting to see how Talia reacted if you told her what Marge had said."

"As a matter of fact, I did tell her," I said abruptly. "I thought she should know."

Sandra's eyes widened.

"Well, good for you. So, what did she say?"

"She was very taken aback. She said Lara was lying. Then she reiterated that the evidence she'd given as a child had been the truth."

"And did you believe her?"

I fell silent. Did I believe her? I had to believe her, the child that had taken my heart so many years ago. Talia had assured me that my faith in her was justified, yet there had been that momentary pause when I'd first spoken, as her dark blue eyes met my own. Had I imagined the expression there, or had I simply had a flashback from the past—to that chilling moment when I had looked into stagnant pools where no life, nor empathy, nor feeling rose from the impervious depths.

Unable to reply, I put my arm around my wife's shoulders and gratefully headed for home.

Elizabeth Elwood (www.elihuentertainment.com) is a playwright, mystery writer, and puppeteer with four plays, six books, many short stories, and twenty marionette musicals to her credit. She is a past Derringer nominee and winner of the Crime Writers of Canada Best Short Story in 2022. Elizabeth lives with her husband and their independent-minded tabby cat on British Columbia's beautiful Sunshine Coast.

GETTING BACK INTO HEAVEN
MARCELLE DUBÉ

When I was a little boy, my mother would put me to bed with a lullaby, a kiss, and a promise.

"God's got a special place waiting for you, Jonas. Right there by his side. A special place for a special boy."

That's how I grew up—blessed, certain that God was waiting for me to finish up down here, so I could join him up there.

Then I went to Afghanistan and the door to Heaven slammed shut.

* * * *

Estelle stood on the mini stoop of the kitchen wall tent, hands wrapped around her mug of Bali Blue Krishna, and took in the early Yukon morning. The sun was just coming up over the Selwyn Mountains but the creek was still drenched in night shadow. Barely five-thirty. The pack lunches were ready, but soon she'd have to go back inside and get breakfast started for the crew of eight geologists sleeping in the four wall tents strung along the creek.

The sleeping tents were smaller than the kitchen tent, which was big enough to accommodate two long folding tables with benches at one end and her propane fridge and stove, an L-shaped rough plywood counter and assorted shelves and cupboards for her supplies at the other. There was even room for an aisle between the tables, and enough headroom to walk in without crouching. She and Jonas had built a plywood platform to set the canvas wall tent on. The platform jutted out enough from the door to provide her with a stoop. Not a big one, but big enough for her to stand on and enjoy her coffee.

This was her favorite time of day, when it was just her with the cold morning. Later on, it would be warm enough to work in her T-shirt, but May mornings in the Yukon wilderness meant work boots, jeans, and a lined work jacket over her sweatshirt.

What she wouldn't do for a cigarette right now. But that was one of the terms in her contract—all their contracts—no smoking while they were in the bush. It was just too dry out here.

She twisted her head around and felt a satisfying pop in her neck. Her shoulders and back ached a little. They would feel worse by bed time.

This was her last camp cook job. At almost fifty, she was getting too old for hauling gray water and generators around.

A raven cawed from its perch atop an eighty-foot black spruce. Faint snoring sounded from the nearest tent. Chisholm, probably.

She took a deep breath of the cool air. Wood smoke, from the fire she had lit in the kitchen tent's tiny wood stove. The sun rose a little higher, picking out the wet stones on the bank of the creek, sending tall tree shadows cutting across the water.

There was a haze in the air, she realized. She turned to look at the sky to the north. She could just make out a faint whiff of forest fire smoke now. Her hands tightened on her mug. Her friends in southern Canada laughed when she told them there was a difference between the smell of wood smoke— from a clean fire in a wood stove—and the smell of a forest fire. A forest fire burned everything in its path—green wood, old wood, rotten wood. Garbage, shrubbery, houses, animals.

People.

A twig snapped to her left and she turned, sloshing coffee over her hands.

Jonas Bellechasse rounded the corner of the cook tent, rifle slung across his broad back. The sleeves of his ancient gray sweatshirt were pushed up over muscular forearms. He nodded as he edged by her to go inside the tent.

He was a big man, his six-foot-four-inch frame towering over her by more than a foot. Every time he stood next to her, she had to control an urge to take a step back. The one time he touched her, he had grabbed her arm to steady her when she tripped over a root. Her upper arm had been black and blue for a week. The boy didn't know his own strength.

Not a boy, really. He was older than the geologists snoring away in the tents. She figured he was probably close to thirty. Handsome enough, in a lean, hard-edged way. His skin fit tightly over his frame, as if an internal fire burned all the fat off him before it could settle. Touching him was like touching a brick wall. No give.

At one time, when she was younger, she might have taken him to her bed. But she was older now. Smarter.

* * * *

Bears don't usually bother camps, unless you're sloppy with food. That cook, now, she's not sloppy. She empties out her gray water far from the camp, burns the scraps, keeps the food in airtight containers. Smart.

But I still like to check the perimeter before I doss out and then first thing in the morning. I mark the perimeter so's the bears know this is a human camp and they'd better stay away. I know none of those geologists do it when I'm not in camp and that bothers me. This is bear country.

I like it here. In camp. It's peaceful, except maybe when the generator's on. We're surrounded by millions of acres of black spruce, pine, and aspen trees, with mountain after mountain stretching out to infinity. The nearest town is Ross River and that's an hour away by chopper.

My only other experience of wilderness was Afghanistan, and that was different. Dryer. Harsher. I had to watch for more than bears over there.

I pour myself the last of the coffee from the cook's special batch and sit down at one of the two long folding tables. We got into the habit in that first week, when it was just me and her setting up the camp. She'd make her coffee, then stand outside to drink it, leaving me the rest. We never talk about it.

She doesn't like me.

No, that's not it. She's afraid of me. A little, anyway. I think she knows I wouldn't hurt her. Not on purpose anyway.

* * * *

None of the geologists—kids, really, not a one of them over twenty-three—none of them ever spent any time with Jonas when he was in camp. Estelle didn't think they did it on purpose. All eight of them worked their asses off, tromping through the bush from first thing when they got up to when they stumbled back into camp as the light failed. They came back starving, exhausted, sometimes discouraged, but sometimes carrying samples in their rucksacks. Then they'd sit around the tables, wolfing food down, talking about the rock formation, the soil composition, the vegetation, comparing notes, writing in their little waterproof journals. They'd fall into bed until she woke them the next morning by turning the generator on.

Jonas would sit alone at one end of the table and watch them. Then he'd get up, sling his rifle over his shoulder, and go out.

* * * *

I come into camp at least once a week, with the regular chopper run. I help unload the supplies for the cook and whatever the geologists asked for. I take their samples and place them in the wooden box trays that I built special and keep on the chopper. That's the only time they come near me, when they have to hand over their precious samples, each one identified with a tag tied around it.

Sometimes I stay for a day or two to help repair things, or help the cook fill up the generator, or dig another latrine—whatever needs doing to keep the geologists exploring. That's what the mining company pays me for. They don't care about what happened in Afghanistan. They only care that I'm good at keeping things running.

Sometimes I miss the army.

* * * *

Estelle grabbed the handle of the five-gallon pail and hauled it out from under the pressed wood counter. Three times a day she had to empty the gray water. That was one chore she wasn't going to miss.

The chopper was due mid-afternoon. She hoped the pilot would bring fruit with her order. She was almost out and the boys got cranky without apples in their lunches.

This was the first time in a few years that she was the only woman in camp. Usually at least one of the geologists was a woman. It was always a comfort to her.

Jonas would probably leave on the chopper. He'd already been here two days and two nights.

She smiled a little as she listed her way toward the screen door under the weight of the pail. It wasn't as if he was good company or anything. He never spoke to her unless he had to, except to say please and thank you.

At least he'd been raised with manners.

The walls of the tent bellowed as the wind caught in the heavy canvas. Her order list, trapped under the clipboard on the corner of the counter, fluttered as the wind found the screened window openings. It was a hot wind.

The loud chime of the radio caught her before she could reach the door. She set the pail down with relief and headed to the back of the tent. The radio sat on a tall stand that had shelves stocked with commercial-sized cans of tomatoes, peaches, and fruit salad. A satellite map was tacked to the inside frame of the tent, just above the radio. She toggled the set on and picked up the receiver.

"Goose Camp. Over."

A brief burst of static, followed by, "Goose Camp, this is Team Leader One. We have a medical emergency. Repeat. We have a medical emergency."

Estelle took a deep breath. Shit. "Team Leader One, this is Goose Camp. Specify, please." Chisholm was Team Leader One. Silly to name a leader for a team of two, but someone had to make final decisions.

There was a pause, followed by more static. "Goose Camp, it's Joe. I think he's got a broken leg."

Shit, shit, shit.

"Compound fracture or simple?" she asked, forgetting protocol.

"No bones sticking out," said Chisholm, "but he can't walk."

Estelle thought for a minute. At least the chopper would be here this afternoon. They had to figure out how to get Joe Brechner back to camp or somewhere the chopper could land.

Would it be easier to get Joe and bring him back, or take a chance that the chopper would be able to land closer to where he was?

"Team Leader One, this is Goose Camp," she said, falling back into habit. "Give me your coordinates."

He did and she looked them up on the map. They were three miles from camp, almost. The nearest flat spot was a mile away from them, due north.

"Team Leader One, stay put for now," she said with her best matter-of-fact voice. "I'll get back to you." She took a deep breath. "Chisholm, you remember your first aid?"

"Splint. Keep him comfortable, protect against shock," said Chisholm promptly. "I've jury-rigged a splint, but how do you propose we get him out?"

"Working on it," she said. "Goose Camp, out."

She put the receiver back on its hook and stared down at the pressed wood floor. Each team went out with a first aid kit, but it was a basic kit—nothing that could handle a broken leg. They had to get the boy out of there. Who was closest to Team One?

* * * *

I dream about her sometimes. The Afghan girl. And sometimes she has my mother's face. Those are the times I wake up crying.

* * * *

Estelle grabbed a pen from the shelf beneath the radio and marked Team One's location on the map.

The clipboard dangling from the tent frame by the map swayed as the tent walls shuddered in the wind. Each day, the teams jotted down the route they planned to take. She spent a few minutes working out the coordinates. Radner and Delisle—Team Three—were closest to Team One.

She tuned the radio to Team Three's frequency and picked up the receiver.

"Team Three, this is Goose Camp. Come in." She waited ten seconds and then repeated. "Team Three, this is Goose Camp. Come in, please."

Just as she was about to try again, the radio chimed. "Goose Camp, this is Team Three. Go ahead." Radner's voice.

"Team Three, what is your location?"

Just as Radner replied, the screen door slammed open, startling her into almost dropping the receiver. Jonas stood framed in the doorway, filling it, his expression lost in the glare of the white sky behind him.

"Wind's shifted," he said. "Smoke is moving in. Get on the horn and tell head office."

He turned to go back out and she called out to him. "Jonas, wait!"

Turning back to the receiver, she depressed the button. "Team Three, hold for two." Then she put the receiver down and turned back to Jonas.

"It's Joe Brechner," she said. "Broken leg. Three miles from camp."

Jonas stepped inside and the screen door slammed shut behind him. He leaned down and grabbed the handle of the pail filled with gray water. Then he looked down at her. "I'll get the stretcher and the first aid kit," he said. "Who's closest?"

"Radner and Delisle. I was just talking to them when you came in."

Jonas nodded, then looked over his shoulder at the view through the screen door. His blond buzz cut looked almost silver in the glare. "Get them to rendezvous with Team One," he said. "We're going to need manpower to haul Brechner out of there." He turned back to her. "Then call the others and get them back here. We're probably going to have to bug out."

With that, he opened the door and stepped down to the ground, carrying the pail as if it were filled with foam instead of forty pounds of water.

The door closed behind him and she turned back to the radio, aware of the stink of forest fire catching at her nose and throat.

* * * *

No idea why I grabbed the cook's pail. I guess I'm on autopilot. I empty it in the gray water pit and consider next steps. The chopper's going to be here in a matter of hours. Everybody has to be back at camp by then.

The sky's already white and filmy with smoke. I don't know how much time we have.

The chopper's going to have to make two trips, minimum. Three if we have to pack Brechner onto the chopper on a stretcher. Even if the company sends a second chopper in, it'll have to come all the way from Whitehorse. That's three hours away, minimum.

I leave the pail by the edge of the pit, upside down so it drains. Then I run back to the kitchen tent and rummage around at the back of it, where we keep extra supplies. The molded plastic stretcher is on the bottom, with boxes of canned goods piled on top. I can hear Cook on the blower but I can't tell who she's talking to.

I empty the stretcher, then pull it out. It's going to be a bitch running through the bush with the damned thing, but there's no help for it.

By the time I return to the front of the kitchen tent, Cook's outside, kneeling on the ground and going through the heavy metal box that holds all the first aid supplies. She's already pulled out leg splints, gauze bandages, antiseptic pads. I drop the stretcher next to her and run to the nearest sleeping tent to grab a blanket.

When I return, she's stuffed everything into a backpack. I hand her the blanket and without a word, she rolls it up nice and tight and ties it to the bottom of the pack.

She stands up and I hear her knees pop. She hands me the pack and I'm surprised at how heavy it is.

"There's ten bottles of water in there," she says. "Just in case. The first aid supplies. Pain killers, bug dope. A dozen energy bars." She spares me a quick smile. "And duct tape."

"Good woman." I've already got the radio clipped to my belt, along with my Leatherman and GPS. I'm as ready as I'm going to be.

"Chopper's coming?" I ask.

She nods. "An hour. Maybe a bit longer."

"All right," I say. "Get as many on it as you can, and get out. I'll get the others back here as quick as I can."

She may be old, but she's steady and there's no hesitation in her eyes. "See that you do," she says crisply and helps me strap the pack on.

Then I grab the stretcher and haul ass.

* * * *

Estelle was hauling the barbecue's propane tank toward the fuel drums that she'd pulled away from the helicopter pad when the first team made it back to camp.

Roberts and Choquette stumbled out of the woods, their faces red with exertion. Estelle abandoned the propane tank ten feet from the fuel drums and ran to meet them.

They dropped their packs outside the cook tent and went inside. She hurried after them and found them guzzling water from the stash of bottles by the counter.

It was an hour since Jonas had left and she'd spent it packing all the food away, in case they were gone from camp for a while, disconnecting the propane tank on the barbecue, and shutting off the generator.

As she worked, she kept an eye on the sky, which was disappearing behind an opaque veil of gray smoke. Tendrils seeped into the clearing where their camp stood, and when breathing grew uncomfortable, she wet a tea towel and wrapped it around her nose and mouth.

Now she pulled it off and took a tentative breath. The cook tent still smelled of bacon from this morning, and while she could smell the smoke, it wasn't bad inside.

She was about to ask what they had seen when she got her first good look at them. Their eyes were squinty and red with irritation, and they breathed heavily. Choquette had a rasp to his breathing. Without a word, she pulled two more tea towels out and wet them before handing them over.

Her eyes were irritated, as was her throat. She couldn't imagine how they must feel having trekked through the bush for the last hour.

Roberts downed half a bottle before taking a deep breath and looking at her.

"Chopper?"

"Any minute now," she said, glancing at Choquette. His face was still red, but he seemed to be breathing better. Where were Crabtree and Doucette?

Hadn't they been closer to camp?

"Which one?" asked Roberts.

Estelle blinked. "Which one what?"

"Chopper. Which chopper?"

"The 204. Why?" The Bell 204 was a workhorse of a chopper. It could carry cargo and up to ten passengers.

Roberts and Choquette exchanged a glance.

"What?" said Estelle, alarmed.

"Tell them to send the 204 to get Joe and the others out," said Choquette, his French accent more pronounced than ever. "The 206 won't be big enough. We think the fire has cut off Team Two from camp. They'll have to make their way to Joe and find somewhere up there for the chopper to land."

Estelle shook her head firmly. The 204 needed much more room to land than the 206. If the chopper couldn't find a spot to land up there, the boys would be stranded. "We'll stick to the plan—"

The chirp of the radio interrupted her and she got up to answer it.

"Goose Camp, over."

"Goose Camp, this is Team Two." Crabtree's voice filled the tent. "We have a problem." His voice was a little higher than usual and Estelle's heart sank.

"Go ahead, Team Two," she said calmly. Choquette got up to stand next to her. He stank of smoke and sweat.

"We're cut off," said Crabtree. "We can't get back to camp. We're going to head for Team One's location."

Estelle thought for a moment. "Give me your location," she said and jotted the figures down when Crabtree did.

"Wait one, Team Two," said Estelle. She stood there for a moment, eyes closed, aware that Roberts and Choquette were watching her. It hit her suddenly just how young they were. How young they all were.

Roberts took the pencil and marked Team Two's location on the map, then looked expectantly at her.

She flipped to Jonas's channel.

"Goose Camp to Jonas."

Seconds later, Jonas's voice emerged from the radio, calm and strong.

"This is Jonas."

"Location?" asked Estelle.

Without hesitation, Jonas rattled off his GPS coordinates and Roberts marked them on the map. Jonas was almost at Team One's location. Crabtree and Doucette were farther away, but the flat spot she had tentatively identified earlier was within half a mile of them.

She flipped the dial to channel three.

"Team Three this is Goose Camp. What is your location?"

A moment later, Radner's voice came on. "We're almost at Team One's location."

She nodded to herself, studying the map. Team Three, Team One, and Jonas. That was five. Seven with Crabtree and Doucette. Too many for the smaller chopper, especially if they had to load Joe in on the stretcher.

But she had no idea how old that satellite map was. That flat spot could be covered in trees now. And it didn't look very big to her.

Still, it wasn't as if they had a choice.

Once Jonas got to Team One, they could haul Joe out of there. She would give them the coordinates of the tentative landing spot. Then she had to talk to head office and get them to agree to her plan.

It took almost fifteen minutes, but she got all three teams and Jonas sorted out. By the time she signed off, they could hear the chopper coming in for a landing.

* * * *

The Brechner kid, Joe, looks like he's in shock, and when I see his leg, I understand why. The bone may not have broken the flesh, but it's a bad break and his lower leg is bent at an unnatural angle. Probably both bones are broken. We have to get the kid out before shock kills him.

Chisholm looks up from tending to Joe when I emerge from the trees and he straightens up, trying not to show how relieved he is.

"Jonas," he says, his voice raspy with the smoke.

We're higher up here than at camp, but the smoke is beginning to roll in. Time to get out.

"Team Three should be here any minute," I tell him. "Let's get him into the stretcher."

Chisholm nods jerkily and I wonder if maybe he's in shock, too. One problem at a time.

I drop the stretcher next to Joe and take the backpack off. Joe looks like hell, his face pasty white, his teeth gritted. Still, I've seen worse. Much worse.

Splinting Joe's leg is going to be tricky, what with the bone pressing up against his flesh, but we have to immobilize it or the trip to the clearing may kill him.

With Chisholm's help, I stuff the splint full of sanitary napkins to cushion the leg and carefully strap the splint on. Even as gentle as we are, Joe roars in pain before passing out. Probably just as well. We wrap him in the blanket and by the time we finish strapping him into the stretcher, we can hear crashing and cursing in the bushes.

Chisholm calls out and Radner and Delisle follow the sound of his voice until they stumble into the tiny clearing.

I look them over while Chisholm fills them in on Joe's condition. They're both breathing hard and raspy. Delisle's face is almost as red as his hair, but it's hard to tell with Radner because of his black skin. Their eyes are bloodshot. But they're strong and fit. They have to be to do their jobs. They'll do.

* * * *

The pilot was an ass.

Estelle stood in front of Sully McMann and stifled an urge to throttle the man. He was piloting the Bell 204, the 10-passenger chopper, in spite of her specific—*specific*—request that the company send the six-passenger one to camp and the 204 to pick up the others.

"Come on, Stella," yelled Sully over the sound of the rotor blades whirring slowly over their heads. "We gotta leave now!"

Estelle shook her head. The smoke was much thicker now, and her throat felt raw from it, and every instinct told her to go and go *now*. But she couldn't, not if it meant abandoning the others.

Her bug-out bag was at her feet, all ready to be loaded on. All three of them had packed lightly, and gone through the sleeping tents, trying to figure out what the others would like packed out. Roberts and Choquette were already inside the chopper, waiting, but she knew if she got on, Sully would just ignore her argument and take them back to Whitehorse.

Her only chance was to stand her ground and insist.

"We have to go to the clearing," she shouted, pointing at the piece of paper in her hand with the coordinates. "They won't all fit in the 206!"

But Sully was shaking his head again. "I'm too big to land," he argued. Again. "And it's even worse up there than it is here."

"We can't abandon them," she insisted. "We at least have to try!"

Sully looked down at her. He was about her age, with a ruddy face and laugh lines, and a small beer paunch.

"One pass," he said, holding up one finger. "If there's the least risk to my passengers or my bird, we're out of there."

"Thank you!" She grabbed his arm and squeezed it.

"Don't thank me," he said grimly. "If I can't land, it'll only make it worse for those we have to leave behind."

* * * *

The girl couldn't have been more than fifteen. She was probably younger. I'd seen her in the village—we'd all seen her. With those big green eyes of hers, she stood out from the other villagers. She always walked around wearing a loose orange scarf over her thick brown hair, and loose robes, but nothing could disguise her figure. Her beauty.

The captain, now, he was obsessed with the girl. Always some excuse to leave the base and go to the village, especially when the women were out fetching water from the well, or getting bread from the small bakery. And he always wanted me driving him, even if it meant waking me up after I'd had night duty.

"You scare the bad guys, Jonas," he would say, as if that were funny.

He wasn't a bad guy, the captain. Not really. I think he'd just been in theater too long. He forgot who he was.

It had to be something like that.

* * * *

The moment they were aloft, Estelle understood Sully's concern.

Below them, the whole world was smoke.

* * * *

As soon as we emerge from the woods at the clearing, I know we're in trouble. There is no way the 204 can land here. The clearing's too small, with too many tall trees, even a few growing right in the clearing.

Crap.

We set Joe down and straighten our backs. Radner's almost as big as me, so we took the front of the stretcher, leaving Delisle and Chisholm on the back.

Joe kept coming to, and passing out as we jarred his leg against trees. Once, Delisle dropped his end and we almost dropped Joe too.

The smaller chopper can land here. Probably. But it can only fit six passengers, tops, and we're seven. Or will be, as soon as Crabtree and Doucette meet us.

I grab the radio off my belt and call them.

"Team Two, this is Jonas, come in."

A moment later, Crabtree comes on. "This is Team Two. You there yet?"

"Affirmative," I say. "What's your ETA?"

"Five minutes, maybe," says Crabtree. A spasm of coughing comes through the radio before he shuts off.

I'm sweating and hot, and all I want right now is clean air to breathe. Not going to happen while we're here.

Chisholm comes up to me, stumbling on the uneven ground, and I realize the guy's beat.

"Pain killer," mumbles Chisholm and I take the pack off my shoulders. It's not a good long-distance pack. No hip straps for distributing the weight, no pockets inside, either.

I set it on the ground and crouch, digging through it for the pouch. We gave Joe a T-3 two hours ago. I'm reluctant to give him another one. I'm no medic but that stuff is pretty powerful. I find the pouch and pull out the small bottle with the T-3s, then I pull out my Leatherman and cut the pill in two. Chisholm stares at it for a minute then closes his fist around it.

Then he looks at me. "It's not good, is it," he says, low and rough like he wants to shout but doesn't dare.

I just stare back at him.

* * * *

"I can't see a thing!"

That was Choquette. Leastwise, Estelle thought it was. Accents didn't translate well over the headphones, so it might have been Roberts.

The steady whup-whup of the rotor blades filled her ears, muted by the headphones. This far up, the air was clearer, but below the smoke infiltrated the forest with long, thick streamers of white and gray. Even up here the air stank.

Sully tapped the GPS dial with one long finger.

"We're almost there," he said.

Estelle leaned forward but all she could see was white, with the tops of spruce trees sticking out. Like construction paper Christmas trees and cotton batting.

* * * *

The captain had me park the Iveco outside the village, in the shadow of a bombed-out cluster of houses, long deserted. He told me he was meeting an informant and didn't want the sound of the light support vehicle to wake the villagers. Wait here, he told me. Be quiet.

So I let him go off on his own.

It was so early it was still dark. The sun rose late here, as it had to claw its way past the mountains. I hadn't had a chance to sleep yet. He'd pulled me out as soon as I got back from patrol, before I could even hit the rack.

I shoulda known he was lying. He'd been acting squirrely these past few days. Jumpy. Hadn't even wanted to go to the village until now.

I'd thought he was finally getting over his obsession with the girl.

God help me, I fell asleep.

I fell asleep in the cab of the truck, my head leaning against the door frame, window open even though it was cold. It was always freezing cold at night, and fry-your-brains hot during the day.

I hated the place. I think it hated me right back.

Something woke me up—a noise—and I jumped out of the LSV, landing on my feet with my Sig in my fist before I even realized what I'd heard.

A muffled cry.

It was still dark, but the sky was lightening in the east. I couldn't have slept for more than twenty minutes. I felt groggy and stood there blinking, trying to figure out what was happening.

All I could see was the shape of the house, its broken walls jagged and light against the hills beyond it. The road was hidden by the bulk of the ruins. Behind the house were more destroyed houses, and beyond them the hill rose, covered with scrub brush, cedars and pines.

I stood next to the LSV, trying to gauge where the sound had come from, but all I could hear was the wind through the pine needles. I could smell snow from the high alpine, and gasoline from the LSV. I moved toward the back of the house, watching where I put my feet.

You stay in theatre long enough and you develop a sixth sense for the hinky. Right now, that sixth sense was telling me something was wrong.

I should never have let the captain go off alone. That informant could just as easily be an ambush. I needed to find the captain and get us both out of here in one piece.

In my first week here, I learned to walk silently and not leave a trail. So I cocked the Sig and made my way around the destroyed house, then carefully walked to the next house. It was filled with rubble and rats, but nothing else.

Then I heard a cry, quickly muffled. There. In the last house flush against the flank of the mountain. It had sounded like a woman's cry.

My stomach clenched in horror and my mouth went dry.

I knew.

I unclipped the flashlight from my belt and crept toward the house's yawning door. It was dark in there, but I could hear shuffling and heavy breathing.

For a second, so help me God, I actually debated going back to the LSV and waiting. Pretending I didn't know. Then I turned the flashlight on and swept the interior with the beam.

The captain turned toward me, his expression half startled, half furious. He was on top of the girl, one hand over her mouth. Her hands were tied and her woolen robe was bunched up around her waist. She looked at me, her eyes shiny with tears.

* * * *

"I hear a chopper!" says Crabtree.

He and Doucette finally made it to the clearing, just in time to hear the arrival of the chopper. We can't see it yet, it's still too far, but even at that distance, I know it's the 204, and that this won't work.

I look across at Chisholm and he's staring back at me, eyes red-rimmed, mouth tight with the same knowledge.

* * * *

Jonas's voice came over the earphones, as clear as if he were standing next to her.

"Negative, Sully," he said calmly. "That clearing won't take the 204. You need to get out now."

Estelle could see the group of them clustered in the middle of the clearing. The wind from the rotors kept the smoke at bay, enough anyway that she could see how small the clearing was. How impossible it was.

"Jackson is on his way with the 206," Sully responded calmly. "ETA is ten minutes. He'll get you out."

Yeah, thought Estelle. For the first time in years, tears welled up. *He'll get most of you out.*

* * * *

The 206 lands without a problem. Without crashing, anyway. The sound of it, the wind from its rotor blades beating the air… it all brings me back to Afghanistan, to the day I forgot who I was.

* * * *

The captain is screaming at me to get out while the girl is just screaming, period. I stare at that scene and I know I'll never be able to forget it for as long as I live.

"Get up, Captain," I finally manage to say.

"Jonas, get the hell out of here!" His hips are still grinding into hers and all I can see is his hairy ass and the fear and pain in her eyes.

I bring my Sig up under the flashlight and point both at him. The girl is quietly sobbing now, her cloud of hair dark against the rubble.

"Get up, Captain."

"Get *out*, soldier, before I put the MPs on you!" He's grunting now. Like a rutting pig.

That's when I hit him with the butt of the Sig.

* * * *

There's no way the stretcher will fit inside the chopper, so we take Joe out of it. He passes out from the pain of transferring him inside, even though we're trying hard to be gentle.

I push Radner inside and he sits beside Joe, with Joe's injured leg propped up on his lap. Next I push the others in and they shuffle around until there's only one seat left. The pilot, Jackson, catches my eye and there's a sick look on his face. I ignore him and turn to Chisholm, who's still on the ground next to me.

"Get in!" I yell to be heard over the sound of the rotor.

"You get in!" he says. "There's one seat left!"

In spite of the fact that I'm older, as blond as he is dark, and I'm taller and outweigh him by at least fifty pounds, at that moment he reminds me of me. It's there in the set of his jaw, the determination in his brown eyes.

There's no time for this. I clap him on the shoulder.

"I know." I lean in so he can hear me more clearly. "I'll make my way back to camp. If the chopper can't come back for me, I'll follow the creek to Ross River."

Chisholm is already shaking his head.

* * * *

In the end, the captain never saw the inside of a courtroom. The MPs never even arrested him, even though I reported him. The commander of the base advised me to let it go, that the captain had been reprimanded and would be reassigned.

I didn't say a word, just watched the commander as he told me. He couldn't meet my eyes. I went back to my rack and threw up.

The next day, I went to find the girl. I don't know what I wanted to do. Apologize, maybe. Make sure she was okay.

I found her house in the village. The men met me outside, their faces stony and angry, but it was the older woman, the only one who could speak halting English, who told me. Her mother.

The girl had killed herself the night before. She had climbed the mountain and thrown herself off. They had found her body thanks to the fluttering of her orange head scarf.

I don't know if she committed suicide or if she was helped. Honor is everything over there, and she had been dishonored.

I went back to camp, found the captain in the mess tent, and I told him. He couldn't look at me.

"Those people—" he began.

That's when I hit him. And I kept hitting him until they pulled me off. If they hadn't, I would have killed him. There was nothing but death in my heart.

* * * *

"You'll never make it, man," said Chisholm, leaning into me.

I shrug. I figure I stand a pretty good chance.

The pilot is gesturing at us. It's time to go.

"Get in, Chisholm," I yell in his ear. "Go. I'll see you back in town."

A look crosses his face, so fast that I have trouble making it out. Despair? Grief?

"Why are you doing this, man?"

I just look at him. Then I smile.

"I'm just trying to get back into heaven."

* * * *

Estelle sat on the pile of bags on the tarmac at the Whitehorse airport and watched the ambulance drive away with Joe Brechner. The boy had not looked good and the EMTs had immediately placed him on oxygen and started him on a saline IV drip.

The company had sent cars to pick everyone up and take them to the hospital to get checked out, but she had refused to go, volunteering to stay with everyone's bags until a car could come and get them and drop them off at the company bunkhouse.

To her surprise, Al Chisholm had decided to stay behind, too. As soon as Sully had refueled, he'd set out again, heading for camp, where hopefully Jonas would be.

And Estelle planned to stay right where she was until Jonas Bellechasse made it back.

Marcelle Dubé's short stories have appeared in anthologies and magazines, including *Black Cat Mystery Magazine, Alfred Hitchcock's Mystery Magazine,* and *Mystery Magazine.* She is best known for her Mendenhall Mystery series, featuring Chief of Police Kate Williams. Her work has been short-listed for the Derringer Award and the Crime Writers of Canada Award of Excellence, which she won in 2021. Find out more at www.marcellemdube.com.

AN IMP IN SPY'S CLOTHING
ROBERT JESCHONEK

Know why I love Lisbon, Portugal, so much? This lunch spot, for one thing.

My table at the edge of a vast terrace overlooks the ancient Alfama district. Orange terra cotta rooftops march down a sunbaked hillside to the sparkling blue Tagus River. The sky overhead is twice as blue, with a hot August sun like a bright gold coin and not a single cloud in sight. My long black hair flutters in the warm breeze, and my tan seems to deepen by the minute.

Lucky me, I get to enjoy this incredible view as I sip the best iced tea on Earth and savor rich *caldo verde* kale soup. I get to feel incredibly re-laxed, just like the waitstaff and the people at the tables around me.

Did I mention I *love* this town?

Being here is my number one joy in life. *Staying* here is my top prior-ity. Why *else* would I do the things I do?

For example, see that straw shoulder bag lying on the table? When I finish, pay, and walk away, the bag will be on my shoulder…but the ma-nila envelope inside it will stay behind. It will "accidentally" slip out, and someone I don't know will come and pick it up.

Because of that, a few days from now, I—Maricela Valente—will get paid. As a result, I'll be able to pay my bills and stay in Lisbon. *That* is what *I'm* working for. *This*—this beautiful *view*—is why I do what you might consider some *questionable* things.

Though *I* just consider them *fun*.

* * * *

Would you call me a *spy* or an *agent* if you spent a day with me? I highly doubt it.

I do some of the things that spies do, but I never actually *spy* on anyone (except this one guy I call *Chesty* or *Kris Chestofferson*, for reasons that will soon become clear).

Allow me to demonstrate. After lunch, I walk through the Alfama, winding my way through the steep cobblestone alleys. Dogs yap, people laugh, and laundry flaps overhead on lines strung between wrought iron balconies.

At exactly fifteen minutes after one o'clock (1300 hours, if you want to get Euro about it), a gray-haired woman emerges from a doorway and hobbles toward me. So, what do I do?

I bump her with my shoulder on the way past, making her stumble on the cobblestones.

It might not have looked like much, but we just accomplished a little mission there. Ever hear of a "brush pass?" One person passes something to the other, and you'll never see it if they're good enough.

Which we are…but guess what? Nothing got passed. It was all for effect, to make whoever's watching think something might be up. It was meant to distract the local intelligence community from something more important. Or to make them *think* there's something important we're distracting them from.

Just like a *hundred percent* of what I do for a living.

* * * *

Continuing my rounds, I stop outside a coffee shop and use the front window as a mirror. Taking off my sunglasses, I primp my long hair, tossing and arranging it over the front and back of me.

Turning right, then left, I admire my sleek profile, expertly framed in a tight yellow tank and white skirt. A middle-aged guy with a gray goatee in the coffee shop likes what he sees and gives me a friendly thumbs-up.

I pull out my phone and snap a photo of my smiling reflection, which for all you know might be capturing an image of some secret message on the other side of the glass.

Though I can assure you, it isn't. It never *is*. *My* job is to make it *look* like I'm up to no good when all I am is a *decoy*. To *act* like a professional spy—brushing the wrong people, leaving empty packages at dead drops, having cryptic conversations—but never coming in contact with any sensitive information.

Does this sound like it might be a blast? Then you are absolutely right. *Especially* when I know I've attracted attention, and it's wild goose chase time…like right now.

Leaving the coffee shop, I scoot around the corner and hop on an old-fashioned yellow tram that's waiting there. I get the last seat, a wooden bench near the back, so the Asian girl who's been not-so-secretly *following* me has to *stand* when she gets on board.

For the next ten minutes, I laugh my ass off (to myself) as Tram 28 jolts its way up one practically vertical hill and down another, leading to some slapstick as my supposed tail white-knuckles the handholds and struggles to stay on her feet.

She's a newbie, I can tell, and fresh out of her early twenties. Oh, the fun I could have with *her*, as I've had with so many others in my three years at large in Lisbon.

But I settle for getting off in the Baixa district and losing her in the crowd in Rossio Square. I do celebrate, though, with a little glass of *ginja* cherry liquor in a nearby bar.

It's times like this when I love my life the most, when my heart's still pounding from some mischief I've done. I feel *alive* and on the *edge,* though my tricks are never deadly, and I'm never in danger.

I've heard people like me called *confetti.* Throw a handful, and it's hard to see what's *really* going on.

But I think of myself more as an *imp,* a little devil stirring up trouble and getting away with it. If the people I work for benefit from the awesome life I'm leading, I'm glad…*whoever* they are.

* * * *

Where *are* you, Kris Chestofferson?

Every day except Monday, I can find him at 1500 hours near the Santa Justa Lift in the Baixa District. Today's Saturday, but he doesn't seem to have shown up.

I go straight over from Rossio Square, and the time is right, but he's nowhere in sight. He isn't doing his usual bit, mingling with the horde of tourists waiting to ride the historic elevator, built in the late 19th century.

I keep looking, though, flashing the signal that lets him know it's me— blowing bubbles with a big piece of purple chewing gum. It's the only way to be sure he knows it's me, no matter what I look like. (Have I mentioned I disguise myself constantly?)

Not that Chesty and I have ever said more than a few words to each other. We work for different sides, after all. (At least I *think* so.) Not that we've had a *thing* going or ever *could.*

But I'd *like* to. And when I look in his eyes, I get the feeling *he* might like to as well.

Disappointed, I pop my latest bubble, then have a last look around. Someone (not Chesty), grabs my ass, and I trip him for his trouble, sending him bellyflopping onto the cobblestones. I spit my gum at his greasy blond ponytail for good measure and sashay off to ride the underground train home and get my afternoon orders.

* * * *

I've never been to Sintra. It's about half an hour from Lisbon, but I've never been there.

Though according to my orders, that's about to change.

At home in my cozy apartment in Bairro Alto, down by the Tagus River, I cuddle up with my trusty shortwave radio for my daily dose of creep-out. Switching it on, I tune to the frequency for today, which I know from a schedule transmitted in a previous broadcast.

Today's transmission starts with a weird tune that sounds like it's coming from a ghostly calliope: *Doo doo, dee dee, dah dee dah doo dum,* repeated several times.

Then, the voice of a woman with a British accent repeats a series of numbers: *Five, one, eight, four, zero. Five, one, eight, four, zero.*

Next, a man with a French accent says the word *Mandelbrot*…and the super-creepy music pipes in again.

Welcome to the wonderful world of *numbers stations.* Here's why it's the best messaging system ever for spies (and imps) in the field. *Anyone* can *hear* it, but only someone with the right cipher key can *understand* it. Best of all, you can't be traced by listening in; there's no trail, as there is with e-mail or phone calls, because you're just tuning in a radio station.

Six, nine, five, two, seven. Six, nine, five, two, seven.

I write it all down and translate while munching a burnt custard tart left over from breakfast. (If anyone ever asks, *yes* you *want* one.) And that's where Sintra comes in.

After three years of *drop this, pick up that, bump into her at such and such a time, yodel on the Águas Livres aqueduct at dawn,* I get an order to *take a trip.*

"Huh." I double-check the decryption, and it all comes out the same. I'm supposed to be at a hotel room in Sintra tomorrow at 900 hours.

No further explanation is provided. I listen to the numbers station again, and nothing else comes through.

So, it's Sintra, here I come.

I am *not* happy about this. I'm sure Sintra's a perfectly nice place, but *Lisbon* is my *jam.* If I'd wanted to go out of town, I would've traveled *somewhere* in the three years I've *been* here.

Maybe, if you'd spent some time in the shit-stain town where I grew up in central Pennsylvania, USA—a dump where the only things worse than the gloomy weather were the alcoholic painkiller addicts who "raised" me with their razor-sharp tongues and the backs of their hands—you would get why I like to stay put in this heavenly land of perfect views and delish custard tarts.

Plus which—you got me—I'm a little *worried.* Impish fun in the city I know and love is one thing, but a mystery field trip to a place I've never *been* to?

I'm no spy. I'm *confetti,* remember? Human *static.* Part of the *churn.* In the intelligence game, I'm a glorified *extra*…so why all of a sudden are they calling me off the bench?

* * * *

It's a beautiful sunny morning when the sexy blonde in the red dress rolls her rental car down the narrow, winding road into Sintra. Let's call her Jacinta Delgado.

Though Maricela Valente will also do just fine. I *told* you I disguise myself constantly, remember? When it comes to throwing surveillance off track, changing appearance often is a *good* thing.

This is the one part of the job where my old life in Pennsylvania pays off. Working as a hairstylist back then prepped me well for a life of constantly changing makeovers. Ray, the guy who recruited me, didn't mention it, but I think it's one of the reasons he liked me for the job in Lisbon in the first place. (That, and the fact I speak fluent Portuguese. Thank you, *Vovó* Lucia—Grandma—the one decent human being in my abusive family circle.)

Jacinta, Maricela—whatever my name is, I keep a firm grip on the wheel through the hairpin curves. I could do without the tour bus slowing things down, but eventually it turns off into a parking lot, and the town opens up below me.

I gasp when I first get a look at it—the *view*, that is. An endless sprawl of countryside fans off in the distance, one green hill and checkerboard field after another.

I can see all this so well because of the way the town wraps around the mountainside. Colorful old buildings are stacked in staggered tiers along the switchback streets, leaving maximum uncluttered airspace in the direction of the view.

Looks like a nice place, I think, as I follow the directions to the hotel from memory. (GPS, which leaves a digital trail, is *not* the fave of spy types or imps in spies' clothing.)

Looping around the tightly wound streets, I find the hotel—the *Os Lusíadas*—in the lower end of town. The place consists of three boxy, two-story buildings clustered together, each with pale yellow walls and faded red shutters.

I park my car, a compact silver Citroen, around the side of the building on the left, tucked under a strawberry tree. It's finally time to find out what this little vacation is all about.

Locking the car, I walk to the nearest door on the ground floor—Room 7. Am I nervous? What do *you* think? It's one thing brushing some person in a public place—quite another knocking on a hotel room door *way* outside my comfort zone.

But knock I do. I have my orders, after all.

I hear voices from inside the room, and the doorknob turns. When the latch clacks out of the jamb and the door eases inward, a single dark eye stares out at me from the crack, under the chain.

"Yes?" The voice is high-pitched, female.

"Mandelbrot is here." I use the code word embedded in my orders from the numbers station.

The dark eye narrows, then disappears as the door slams shut. I hear the chain slide out of its track, and the knob turns again.

This time, the door opens all the way—and I go speechless. Whom do you think I'd be least likely to see standing there in the doorway of Room 7?

If there was a list, the Asian girl from Tram 28 would be near the top of it.

She doesn't smile as she steps aside and ushers me in. Does she hold a grudge for my little maneuver on the tram?

The thought passes quickly when I have a look around. Another question comes to mind instead when I see the other occupants and contents of the room:

WTF?

"Hullo, Mandelbrot." The gray-haired lady I brushed in the Alfama yesterday steps up, though she's not as old as I thought when I brushed her. "Try this on." Her accent is Irish. She has an article of clothing folded over her arm, and she holds it out to me.

If you think I'm confused by this, you should see my face when the guy who grabbed my ass yesterday at the Santa Justa Lift limps over to join us. "Want your gum back?" he says in a Swedish accent. When he turns his head, I see there's still residue from my bubble gum in his greasy blond ponytail.

"Let me guess. Your mind's blown." Someone else approaches—the middle-aged guy with the gray goatee from the coffee shop. His accent sounds like a cross between Russian and German. "Well, get used to it." Taking the clothing from the gray-haired woman, he unfolds and holds it up. "Now let's see if this fits."

Only then do I see it's a vest festooned with explosive packets and wires.

My stomach twists, and a chill shoots up my spine. *It's a suicide vest.*

* * * *

Say you're unarmed and outnumbered, and someone tells you to put on a suicide vest. Looking around, you see it's not the *only* suicide vest in the room, and the vests aren't the only *weapons* at hand. There are assault rifles and ammo clips on the bed, tables, dresser, and floor.

Do you A., put on the vest? B., refuse to put it on, grab an assault rifle, and fight your way out of there? Or C., freeze like an imp in the headlights of a speeding truck?

If you didn't pick C., you don't know me *at all*.

"Relax, Mandelbrot." Gray goatee guy steps toward me with the vest. "We've *all* done it."

I take a step back, though I'm not sure what my next move will be.

Just then, the gray-haired woman touches his shoulder. "She has a lot to wrap her head around, Pythagoras. Maybe it would help if we lay it all out for her."

"You're right." Pythagoras nods. "Euclid, get her the confirmation. We all need to be on the same page."

The Asian woman brings me a sheet of paper covered with rows of alphabetical characters. It's an encrypted message, the kind I periodically receive back in Lisbon.

How do I know it's authentic? I'm about to find out.

I pull a folded slip of paper from my bra. Where better to keep the key for decoding a secret message? "Could somebody give me a pen?"

Pythagoras pats his pockets and turns to the gray-haired woman. "Descartes?"

Descartes grabs a pen from a desk and hands it over. Sitting on the edge of the bed, I get to work deciphering—using my key, what they call a *one-time pad* (because it can be used only once), to unravel the message.

Each letter in the message corresponds with a number. According to the one-time pad, I have to subtract a certain number from that first number to get a *third* number, which I then convert to a letter of the alphabet.

When I finish, I wish I hadn't. I have never received orders like this in my life, though I don't know how smart it would be to tell my hosts that.

The syntax and code words don't lie. That doesn't mean *I* can't.

"Okay." I keep myself calm and steady as I put down the pen. "All done." Nodding, I fold up the paper with the orders I've deciphered and stuff it into my bra with the one-time pad.

"Good," says Pythagoras. "Then we're on the same page?"

"Absolutely." I get up and head for the door. "To start with, I have to pick up a dead-drop at Pena Palace."

"Is that so?" Pythagoras nods at the door, and Euclid moves to block it. "It doesn't say anything about staging a *terrorist attack* at the *National Palace of Sintra* at 1930 hours this evening?"

That's *exactly* what it says, but I shake my head. "I guess I have a different role in the op."

"We *know* that's not true," says Pythagoras. "*Our* orders *told* us so."

"Five rifles." Greasy blond ponytail gestures at the weapons laid out around the room. "Five vests. And one, two, three, four,"—He counts out the people.—"*five* operatives."

"Can't argue with Fibonacci." Pythagoras shrugs. "Like it or not, we're *all* in this clown car till the end."

"But if it makes you feel better," says Fibonacci, "you only have to blow your vest if you get *caught. Probably.*"

* * * *

At least they let me use the bathroom. I hide out in there for a while, trying to keep myself from completely falling apart.

So, this is what it's all come to. Three years of imping around Lisbon, living the sweet life…and *boom.*

I don't remember Ray, my recruiter, warning me that something like this might happen someday, back when he recruited me in my hometown. Would it have made any difference if he *had?* Getting out of Pennsylvania was worth the risk and then some to me.

It was like a fairy tale to me, at the age of twenty-five—this handsome thirtysomething guy chatting me up at a bar one night, offering me a new beginning. How would I like to be a *spy?* All expenses paid, from passport to airfare to food and lodging.

Ray said he was in town for a relative's funeral, but he was always in recruiting mode, looking for someone (like me) with that special some-thing. Was he CIA? KGB? Corporate? I never knew and didn't care. As long as I could live like an imp in heavenly Lisbon, I was fine with what-ever.

Who knew that whatever could kick my ass *this* hard? Now here I am, and one of the terrorists keeps knocking on the bathroom door, calling me by my code name.

"Mandelbrot? It's Descartes. May I come in?"

I take a deep breath to calm myself, then reach over and unlock the door. "Okay." I'm fully dressed, just sitting on the toilet seat lid.

Descartes smiles as she closes the door behind her. "Crazy situation, huh?"

I nod. It's the understatement of the century.

Descartes looks in the mirror, fixes her short gray hair. "I'm guessing this is your first potluck?"

"Potluck?" I frown.

"It's when different intelligence services with a common goal pitch in manpower for the same op. It's not unusual for the assets to be low-level or discards to minimize traceability."

Low-level. That sounds about right, but… "Discards? We're discards?"

Descartes shrugs. "It's nothing personal, I'm sure. We're just 'assets' to them, remember?"

It's something I haven't thought about much between imp tricks and burnt custard tarts. "I didn't sign up to kill people and blow myself up."

"Sure, you did. We all did." Descartes washes her hands in the sink, then dries them with a towel. "We serve at the discretion of our respective sponsors."

"But *why?* Why this *attack?*"

"Your guess is as good as mine," says Descartes. "Maybe they think a fake ISIS strike will drum up support to fight the real thing? Maybe it's a distraction from something bigger happening elsewhere? Who knows?"

"Doesn't sound much like spy work to me."

"Maybe someone else is doing the *real* spy work. Maybe we're just making it possible. We don't see the big picture from way down here." She points at the floor. "So, look, are you going to be okay? If not, we need to make other arrangements."

The way she says it tells me what my answer has to be. "Yeah." I rise from the toilet.

Descartes pats my shoulder. "If it makes you feel any better, the palace will be closed to tourists when we go in. Casualties should be minimal."

"Good." I say what I have to, playing along. "Thanks for the talk."

"Anytime." Descartes smiles and opens the door. "You're not so bad, when you're not *bumping* me too hard on the *brush pass.*"

* * * *

A digital clock on the nightstand blinks the time in blue numbers. If only I could stop 1930 hours from racing toward me. I have never been so terrified in my life.

It takes all I can do to keep from shaking as the others teach me how to handle an assault rifle. We study maps of our target, the National Palace of Sintra, and I feel sick every time they talk about what we're going to do there.

Then, around 1900, it's time to suit up. I swap my red dress for baggy gray coveralls with a patch for a cleaning company (*Tudo Limpo,* "Everything Clean") on the left chest.

Underneath, I wear the vest. It's not that heavy, but it *feels* like it weighs a ton. Having it on makes my blood turn to ice.

Especially when Pythagoras explains how to blow it using the hand switch, and Fibonacci tells me about the failsafe. "Once the clips lock, if anyone tries to remove it the wrong way, it will blow." Grinning, he fastens three buckles down the front of the vest. "And the clips are now locked."

As I zip up the coveralls, I feel like I might blow without any help from the vest.

"One more thing," says Fibonacci. "Failsafe number two is on a timer.

One way or another, if one of us doesn't disable the countdown, you blow at 2030 hours."

"Insurance is a good thing," says Pythagoras. "Don't you think?"

* * * *

By the time we load up the Tudo Limpo van (guns stowed in cleaning carts and garbage bins), I'm so scared that I'm almost ready to flip the switch on my vest and be done with it. If I had any real courage, I would do it just to stop these people and whoever they're working for—whoever *we're* working for.

Everyone is quiet as Pythagoras drives us through the winding streets. At one point, he makes a call on an anonymous burner phone, telling someone (police? media?) that a local branch of ISIS is claiming responsibility for the impending attack in Sintra.

Staring out the window, I think of all the things I'll never do again in my beloved Lisbon. I think of having a picnic lunch of *Papo-seco* bread, *Serra de Estrela* cheese, and *vinho verde* wine in the park at Jardim Botto Machado…enjoying a sunset cruise on the Tagus River on a warm August evening…leaving silly surprises in dead drop packages, from candy to gag gifts to crazy fake messages and maps designed to send the recipient running in circles around town. I think of Kris Chestofferson, too, and teasing him in different disguises at the Santa Justa Lift.

Then, to my surprise, I actually *see* him walking down the street. There can be no doubt; that muscular chest is larger than life.

Heart racing, I take care not to give away my interest to the others in the van. But I note Chesty is heading our way, walking briskly toward the National Palace of Sintra, dead ahead.

A little flame of hope flickers in my heart…but it's dim. The time on the dashboard clock reads 1925. The attack starts in five minutes, and my vest explodes, come what may, at 2030. What are the chances, even with Chesty's help, that I can change that sequence of events?

But if I *don't* try, the chance of success is *zero*.

My head spins as Pythagoras parks the van in front of the palace, not far from Chesty's path. Pythagoras tells us to get out and unload—and I realize my moment has arrived.

It's now or never. Before the team gets their guns, before Chesty walks too far away.

Taking the deepest breath of all time, I head for the rear of the van… and keep going. I'm committed.

Don't look back, I tell myself, even when I hear agitated voices behind me. Instead, I stay focused on Chesty and my thoughts of how this is going to play out.

"Hey there!" I hurry over to him in my baggy gray coveralls. "Wait up!"

Chesty frowns, not recognizing me in my blond wig and cleaning crew getup. *"Olá? Sim?"* Hello? Yes?

How long till I get a bullet in the back from my fellow "cleaners?" I try not to think about it. "It's me! Remember?" Moving in close, I lock eyes with him, willing my true self to shine through.

But he gives me nothing.

Just then, I hear the doors of the van slam shut. Glancing over my shoulder, I see the cleaners rushing toward the palace, pushing their carts and bins. The good news is, they've decided not to risk wrecking the op by shooting me. The bad news is, their attack on the palace will come any minute now.

Desperate, I grab Chesty's arm. "I see you *every day* at the Santa Justa Lift. I always chew *purple gum.*" I push my hair back on both sides, exposing more of my face. "Now listen, I need your help!"

Just as I'm starting to think he's *all* chest and *no* brain, it dawns on him. "Ha! Funny meeting *you* here!"

"Not so funny," I tell him. "There's a terrorist attack *in progress* as we speak! You need to call in your people, *whoever* you've got local, *right now.*"

Instantly, he goes on alert. *"Where?"*

My heart hammers as I turn to point at the big, whitewashed building with the conical spires behind us. "The National Palace. They're dressed like me." I unzip enough of my coveralls to show him the bomb vest underneath. "Like *this*, plus assault rifles. Four of them."

Chesty's eyes flare, and he takes off, chattering into his watch in Portuguese. I notice, as he bolts around the van, that he pulls a handgun from between the waist of his pants and the small of his back.

A moment later, three other athletic guys with guns run full-tilt after him from across the parking lot. His people were closer at hand than I knew.

When they leave me there alone, my mind flies to the next order of business. Looking around, I spot a clock on the wall of a nearby building, and I know.

It is 1945 hours. I have 45 minutes to live.

* * * *

What kind of person are you? If strapped to a bomb vest, would you cry like a baby and blow up in the middle of town, where people are numerous? Or would you cry like a baby and get as far away from people as you could?

I'm the *second* kind, though I never knew it until now.

A taxi stops across the street with its available light on. Impulsively, I run toward it, waving for attention.

The driver, a middle-aged black woman wearing a purple and white dashiki, stares at me over her sunglasses. "Where to?" Her accent sounds French or Belgian to me.

"As far from here as you can get in a half-hour. Someplace where I can get away from other people *fast*."

She narrows her eyes. I'm sure she can tell I'm in a panic. "You want to drop off the edge of the world, *oui*?"

"Sounds perfect."

"You have money?"

I pull out a folded stack of bills that came with the outfit—emergency funds in case the op hit a snag.

The driver smiles. "Get in." She switches the light on the taxi's roof to the occupied position. "You may call me Monique."

I fling the door open and dive in. The taxi smells like pot, and I don't care. "I'm Maricela." No need for an alias now.

I don't have much longer to live.

* * * *

If I had time to post a review of Monique online, it would read like this: *A maniac, plain and simple.*

In other words, she's just the kind of driver I need right now.

The taxi hurtles along the winding mountain road like a flame along a gas-soaked fuse, never slowing down. Anything that gets in our way gets passed at a high rate of speed; anything that comes at us head-on has to dodge or be front-ended.

Meanwhile, I huddle in the back, catching glimpses of the rolling countryside through the blur of speed. Mostly, I watch the clock on the dashboard and pray.

2000, says the clock. *2005. 2010.*

"Almost there," says Monique. "The edge of the world."

Wherever we're headed, I'll stop her in five more minutes and run. I don't want to be anywhere near her when I blow…anywhere near *anybody*.

As we flash around a bend, I see a parking lot ahead, and a low building. Beyond those, a stone pillar rises against the sapphire sky, topped with a gleaming white cross.

"Welcome to Cabo da Roca," proclaims Monique. "The westernmost point of Europe. Nothing but a cliff on the ocean past there. As close to the edge of the world as you're going to *get* a half-hour from Sintra."

My heart chops in my chest like a helicopter blade. I throw all my money on the front seat. "Get me as close as you can! Then get the hell out of here!"

Monique obliges. Tourists scatter as she charges through the half-empty parking lot and barrels along the footpath to the monument.

She skids to a stop at the pillar, her rear tire thudding into the stone dais at its base. The time on her dashboard clock is 2025.

Five minutes to go.

"Get out of here as fast as you can!" I shout as I hurl open the door and duck out of the cab.

Dirt and gravel spin out from under Monique's tires as she shoots back out the way we came.

"Everybody get out of here!" Most people have already fled for the parking lot, but I scream the words anyway. "Get far away from me!"

Beyond the pillar, there's a low stone wall, and I clamber onto it. When I look down at what's on the other side, I have a moment of intense vertigo.

Just over the stone wall, a rocky cliff drops hundreds of feet to the sea. I could not have picked a more perfect place for what I need to do.

As I stand there, a stiff wind pummels me, kicking the blond wig from my head. The wig spins off behind me and circles back, whipping out like a soaring gull over the Atlantic Ocean into which I will soon plunge.

There are worse views to end your life with. The scenery is the prettiest I've ever seen—the yellow sun setting on the horizon, casting streamers of red, orange, and gold into the deep blue sky.

Somewhere out there is my old hometown in Pennsylvania. Even now, even with what I'm about to do, I'm still glad I'm not there, but here.

Spreading my arms wide, I take a deep breath. I can't wait much longer.

At least I got to save the day this once, even if it's nothing I ever asked for. I was always perfectly happy being an imp in Lisbon…though I don't think I did so bad as an imp in spy's clothing, do you?

I take another breath. I can still see the golden light of the sunset on my eyelids when I close them. That light and the roar of the ocean wind block out the rest of the world around me.

Which is why I don't hear the approaching motorcycle until it's right behind me.

Turning, I see Chesty leap off the bike and run toward me. "Get down from there!" He holds a wire-cutting tool in one gloved hand.

I wave him off. "It's too late!"

"Not if I snip the right wires in the next thirty seconds!" He flings up a hand, fingers twitching, reaching for me.

And I know I shouldn't take it, but I *take it*, God, I *take it*, wouldn't *you?*

* * * *

Maybe you've read about the attempted attack in Sintra by now. It's been all over the news, after all.

But one thing you *won't* find out from the news is what happened to *me*. You won't find out how Chesty defused the bomb vest with seconds to spare (he's a real whiz with that stuff)…after tracking me to Cabo da Roca (there was a *lot* of surveillance around Sintra that day)…after quickly stopping the terrorist attack with his people in Sintra (which turned out to be a *much* bigger deal than I knew, with a secret meeting of top Euro and US kahunas in the sights of *Tudo Limpo*).

You won't find out anything *about* me on the news, in fact, because I'm not just an imp anymore. I'm on the *down-low,* off the *radar*. It turns out the spy clothes fit, so I'm wearing them full-time these days.

Chesty and his bosses were impressed enough by my actions in the Sintra affair that they recruited me away from my *former* so-called bosses. I didn't have to think too hard about *that* one, after those douches threw me into the potluck *fuster cluck* the way they did.

I almost lost my life. Now I have a new and different one. I won't be playing decoy all the time, staging wild goose chases with nothing at stake.

Not that my life will be *all* different. Today, for example, I'm breaking into a terrorist's apartment and stealing a set of secret plans. Talk about *high-stakes*, huh? Not exactly an *old* me way to spend a morning.

But after that, I'm meeting Chesty—I mean *Gaspar Aguilar*—for paella and *vinho verde* at a certain lunch spot overlooking the Alfama. I think you know the one I mean.

And after *that*…let's just say there's a burnt custard tart with my name on it.

✗

Robert Jeschonek (bobscribe.com) is a *USA Today*-bestselling author. His stories have appeared in *Black Cat Weekly*; *Mystery, Crime, and Mayhem Magazine*; *Punk Noir*; *Yellow Mama*; *Pulphouse Fiction Magazine*; and other publications. His crime tale, "The Messiah Business," was named an honorable mention in *The Year's Best Crime and Mystery Stories*.

LET'S SETTLE THIS

JACK RITCHIE

This story won the $100 2nd prize in the *Chicago Daily Tribune*'s story contest on Saturday, November 6th, 1954. It was never published—until now!

Evelyn Wheatly looked up as the junior Mr. James Vaughan, as yet unlisted in the law firm of Vaughan & Bensen, came to her desk. "I like walking in the rain," she said.

"I hate it," Jimmy Vaughan said. "Besides, my raincoat leaks."

"I love to travel," Evelyn said, trying again.

Jimmy picked up the briefs Evelyn had finished typing. "Late at night when I hear the lonesome whistle of a freight train, I have an overwhelming compulsion to remain exactly where I am."

He paged through the sheets. "It's apparent that we have absolutely nothing in common. Cease and desist."

Evelyn tilted her blond head for thought. "I'm committing myself first, which leaves you a way out. Let me put it this way. Do you or do you not like onions on your hamburgers?"

Jimmy smiled triumphantly. "I don't eat hamburgers." And then Mr. James Vaughan, Jr., who didn't mind walking in the rain, liked a moderate amount of travel, and was enthusiastic about hamburgers with onions, turned and went into his father's office.

The senior Vaughan accepted the briefs. "That's a good boy," he said.

Jimmy sank into a chair. "This may shock you, Dad," he said. "But I know where the courthouse is, and I can talk as loud as any other lawyer. I have the wild idea that you can trust me with something besides making out wills."

"Just sit there and absorb experience," Mr. Vaughan said. "In a moment I'll think up some sage advice."

Mr. Vaughan read the briefs and said, "Hmm!" wisely several times. Then he put them aside and woke Jimmy from a reverie that might have been a doze.

"Speaking of Evelyn," he said, "why don't you marry her? Speaking for myself, it's all I can do to keep from whistling when I look at her. And I'm a married man, you know."

Jimmy got up. "I suggest I go out to lunch," he said.

* * * *

When Jimmy returned to the office at one, he noticed a large vase of roses on Evelyn's desk.

"Look what I got," Evelyn said. "Want to read the card?"

"It's a trick," Jimmy said. "You sent them to yourself. I refuse to get jealous."

"I met him last night," Evelyn said. "He's calling for me at quitting time. Notice the dreamy look in my eyes?"

"It's no use," Jimmy said stubbornly. "I see through it all. A brother. Possibly a nephew."

Evelyn rolled paper into her machine. "Now run along and deliver a writ or something."

His father looked up as he entered the office. "Here's something you might be able to handle. A Mr. Hanson got arrested for speeding. I told him to plead guilty and pay the ten-dollar fine, but he wants to make a case out of it."

Jimmy sighed and sat down to study the details. At five o'clock he woke and stretched. He walked into the outer office and promptly stopped in his tracks.

The man helping Evelyn into her coat was no brother of hers, nor nephew either. Jimmy recognized him as Eddie Conley, one of his classmates in law school.

Jimmy went back into the office and began to think.

* * * *

In the morning Traffic Court, Jimmy did his preoccupied best. Mr. Hanson was found guilty and fined twenty-five dollars and costs.

That afternoon Jimmy studied his frown in the mirror in his dad's office.

His father observed sympathetically and wondered whether he should put his arm around his son's shoulders. "Never mind," he said finally. "Hanson's case was hopeless anyhow."

"Who's Hanson?" his son inquired absently.

"That's it. Try to forget." Mr. Vaughan examined some papers on his desk. "Now here's something that should turn out better. Fellow named Conklin ran over one of my clients. My client is considerably miffed, and he wants ten thousand dollars." He chuckled gleefully. "Watch how I handle it, boy. I bet we settle for nearly a thousand."

Jimmy listened with minimal interest and then wandered out of the office and up against Eddie Conley.

"Nice to see you again, Jimmy," Conley said. "I heard you were in court today."

Jimmy blushed for himself and then glowered as he noticed that Evelyn watched them.

"I'm representing Conklin," Eddie said. "Is your father handling the case?"

"I'm handling it," Jimmy said fiercely. "We'll sue. I'll take it to the Supreme Court if necessary."

Conley smiled. "My client, while not admitting any responsibility, nevertheless would like to settle this matter amicably. He thinks that five hundred dollars should cover the matter nicely."

"Ha!" Jimmy said, his lip curling in contempt.

Conley laughed professionally. "Perhaps we might make it a thousand. But that's the absolute limit."

Jimmy folded his arms across his chest and became bored. "Ten thousand. Cash, check, or money order."

For fifteen minutes he leaned against a desk and yawned away all offers until the bid stood at five thousand. At that point he allowed himself to be convinced and led Conley into his father's office for the drawing up of the necessary papers.

When Conley was gone, Jimmy swaggered over to Evelyn's desk. "I feel confidence throbbing within me," he said.

"You were magnificent," Evelyn said.

"I know," Jimmy admitted. "Is Conley supposed to pick you up again tonight?"

"Naturally," Evelyn said. "I think he's handsome, don't you?"

"You are on the verge of getting fired. So, watch it," Jimmy said evenly. He put both hands on her desk and leaned forward. "Fifteen minutes before he's due to call for you, you and I will leave for dinner together. The time element is important because he's bigger than I am."

Evelyn looked into his eyes and smiled. "You do realize what this will probably lead to?"

"Too well. But I'm game," Jimmy said. "My intentions are honorable, but interesting."

He leaned forward somewhat more.

* * * *

Beside the keyhole of his office door, Mr. Vaughan waited a minute more before he got to his feet. "Never could understand why women close their eyes when they're being kissed." He looked over the Conklin agreement, tore it up and threw it into the wastepaper basket.

He hobbled to the phone and dialed his printer.

"That's right," he said. "A new letterhead. It's Vaughan, Bensen, & Vaughan now. My boy passed both tests. And while you're at it, Mr. Conley, thank your boy, Eddie. I'll throw some business his way when I can. With that acting ability, he ought to make a great lawyer."

✗

www.ingramcontent.com/pod-product-compliance
Lightning Source LLC
Chambersburg PA
CBHW050830180626
46814CB00004B/1550